78 KEYS

Visit us at www.boldstrokesbooks.com

By the Author

Wind and Bones

78 Keys

78 KEYS

by

Kristin Marra

2011

78 KEYS

ISBN 13: 978-1-60282-222-1

THIS TRADE PAPERBACK ORIGINAL IS PUBLISHED BY
BOLD STROKES BOOKS, INC.
P.O. BOX 249
VALLEY FALLS, NY 12185

FIRST EDITION: MAY 2011

CREDITS
EDITOR: CINDY CRESAP
PRODUCTION DESIGN: STACIA SEAMAN
COVER DESIGN BY SHERI (GRAPHICARTIST2020@HOTMAIL.COM)

Acknowledgments

A writer is nothing without her consultants, most of whom go unpaid and are rewarded by a paltry mention in the "Acknowledgments" page. A giant thanks to the following consultants.

Lucille Gauger and Lisa Greenberg, my medical experts.

Gary Tucker, a specialist in Underground Seattle lore.

Lynn McNamer, security CEO.

Rachel Zakalik, Yiddish maven and world's best personal trainer.

Lisa Brodoff and Lynn Grotsky, top-drawer beta readers and Yiddish critics.

A special thanks to my partner Judith, who will call bullshit when she reads it. Love you, honey.

And thanks to my fabulous daughter Rachel, who has learned (mostly) not to bother Mom when she's writing.

And finally, my deep gratitude to all my Jewish in-laws. Your warm acceptance of me into the extended mishpacha gave this shiksa the chutzpah to write this book.

A word about Yiddish. I've learned that the English spelling of Yiddish words is a minefield of disagreement. Each expert insists that his or her spelling is the correct one. After several weeks of trying to pin down the correct spelling of Yiddish words, I threw up my hands and said, "Enough, already!" I went basic. For most words, I referred to the delightful *The Joys of Yiddish* by Leo Rosten. A few spellings I deferred to the loudest voice. If you have a quarrel with any of the Yiddish spelling, it's my responsibility, but please have some *rachmones*, or pity.

Dedication

This book is dedicated to my mother, Helen Jeanette Marra, who is reading this from the emerald golf course in the sky. Wish you were here, Mom.

CHAPTER ONE

T he hallway was deserted. Half-lit in gray shadow. I knew this place, didn't I?

The office doors that lined the marble hall were locked for the night, their opaque windows darkened. Waist-high ceramic pots cupping giant plastic rubber plants were situated between the doors to give the hall an illusion of warmth. I shivered as I watched her crouch behind one of the pots, hiding like a terrorized child. Her blond head shook while buried into her knees.

The door from the stairway access crashed open. A bulldog of a man lumbered in. The veins in the side of his neck accentuated the swastika tattoo half-visible, as if it crawled from under his collar. He gazed around, his little eyes alert for any movement.

Click. Clink. She dropped her activated cell phone into the pot. He didn't see that, but he heard the sound. He grinned, showing straight white capped teeth that contrasted with his swarthy cruel face.

"Gotcha, bitch." His voice was softer than his face, girlish almost.

When she stood to face him, I marveled at her naïve bravery. Faster than his bound muscles should have allowed, he hoisted one of the huge pots and hurled it at her. Her hands covered her head against the impending lethal blow.

❖

The vision evaporated. I was looking at her, Laura Bishop, but she was no longer in the hall or in mortal danger. Instead, she sat in front of me. One of my tarot clients, one of those who arrived dubious and would leave dubious and pissed off. I'd had enough doubters in my practice to recognize them and still not let them deter the process.

I looked at the tarot cards spread on the small table in the anonymous hotel room. I wasn't surprised to see the image glaring at me from one particular card. A body sprawled facedown, blood oozing from wounds caused by swords quilling the corpse's back. The Ten of Swords: betrayal.

"Ms. Bishop, do you see that card there, in the future position?" Disturbing images could be upsetting to clients, so I always addressed them immediately. Waiting only made clients focus on them to the point of missing anything else I had to say.

"Uh, yeah, I do, Ms. Rosten. Do you psychic folks throw those things in there to scare your clients into coming back? Because, trust me, it won't work." One side of her jaw twitched as she tossed her accusation.

"You may call me Devorah, or Dev, if you like. And, no, we don't create such cards to manipulate clients. In fact, that card makes rare appearances. So I suggest we discuss it for a moment before we move on."

"Yes, let's." She sat back in her chair as if waiting to be entertained but not expecting much. My work was rarely entertaining, but she wasn't ready to swallow that piece of information and probably not the rest of it either.

"Well, you have a Ten of Swords there, and tens show up when stagnation is occurring. Often a client is complacent, not really attending to a situation that demands attention." I had a bad feeling, a dreadful foreboding for this dazzling woman. That vision of the thug proved she required my "extra" services beyond the little card reading, but how to sell her on the idea?

"And what situation are you referring to, Ms. Rosten?"

I glanced again at the cards and saw the Two of Cups. This was not going to be easy, probably impossible, judging from the hostility she was mustering. She had informed me that she was an attorney, so I wasn't willing to engage in a verbal argument with her.

"The Two of Cups usually means a relationship, generally of lovers. Coupled with the Ten of Swords and other, uh, impressions, this will not end well." I knew she wasn't ready to hear I had visions whenever I gave readings. In this case, I was grateful I wouldn't have to share what I'd seen with the swastika-neck guy. I even hated saying the word "swastika." Some words don't glide off my Jewish tongue.

Her fingers were tapping the chair arms. "Did I ask you about any relationship, Ms. Rosten? If I had, then you could talk about it; otherwise, stick with my law practice, please."

"I just think you should know that this guy…"

"I'm a lesbian, Ms. Rosten. There is no guy. Can we move along? My friend Margaret said you were good; now show me. Tell me about my law practice and my plans to open my own firm. Stick with that and I won't feel like I've wasted Margaret's overpriced birthday present to me. Okay?" Beauty coupled with a galvanized backbone. I liked it. I liked her. But she was a client, and my costly tarot reading was her birthday present.

"Right. If that's what you prefer." I kept my breath even and looked for any pentacles, symbols of work and money, in the spread. "There's the Knight of Pentacles, Ms. Bishop. Knights usually are on a quest. They work hard. That's probably you. See those plowed fields? They mean your work will pay off..."

I rambled on about how her law practice would be a ripping success, that she'd have to avoid overworking. However, my mind was really back in that hallway watching the brute of a man throw a giant ceramic pot at her head. That was going to happen to Laura Bishop. I couldn't tell when, maybe in ten days, maybe ten years, but it would happen. And there was nothing I could do to help her. I was sure she would reject my offer of *enhanced* services.

When she was ready to leave, she shook my hand. "Thanks, Ms. Rosten. I liked what you said about my professional future. Let's hope you were accurate. As for the other situation you mentioned, please forgive my anger. I'm under some pressure these days and would rather not discuss my private life. Anyhow, it was nice meeting you."

"Likewise, Ms. Bishop, and if you need any further... consultation, here is my card." I handed her my business card and hoped she'd call. She would need me someday. She dropped the card in her oversized cloth bag.

I stood at the window of the downtown Seattle hotel room and watched her exit the building. Her orange bag kept her in my sight longer than the drizzling rain would usually allow.

After Laura Bishop's tarot reading, I followed her career for years. She resigned from the prestigious Meyers, Gaines, and Stratton and started her own firm she called Bishop and Associates. I learned that her offices were located in the historic Smith Tower. I had been in the Smith Tower on several occasions and realized the hallway I'd seen in the vision where Laura was attacked was a Smith Tower hallway. She would be harmed there.

Her public career entailed her representing clients in high-profile divorces and family custody battles. She also offered many pro bono hours per week in defense of abused children, and she led charitable drives for safe houses for abused families. I read every article about her in the Seattle papers, both general news and gay news. I was enthralled by her, and she appeared to be single. She was in extreme danger, but only I knew it.

I would not do the research into her possible nemesis since she hadn't requested my help. Someday she would need more from me, my extra services. I both hoped for and dreaded seeing her again. She unsettled me in a way other clients never do.

❖

Several years before the session with Laura Bishop, my "enhanced" services began from what I thought was a hallucination. It was the first time I glimpsed the future.

I had spread the cards for a well-to-do client and settled in for the interpretation. Without warning, I found myself in a motel room, watching my unclothed tarot client. She was having sex with a man half her age. A boy really, maybe sixteen years old. They were loud and exultant. I grabbed the dresser to steady myself, and zing, I was back sitting in front of the now fully clothed and silent client. The worn familiar tarot cards were spread innocuously on the table before us. Each image on every card whispered potential meaning to me, but the Five of Pentacles held my attention. The card, sometimes interpreted as wretchedness and alienation, told all I needed to know about the future of my client and her boy lover.

The client was watching me with delicious expectance, waiting for the cards to reveal her prospects.

I coughed. "Oy, that was interesting."

"What? What did you feel…see?" Anxiety tightened her face, but it didn't match the apprehension I struggled to hide.

"Is there a younger man in your life? Someone you may be…attracted to?" I had no idea how to broach this. I'd never had a vision while reading cards, but I'd studied enough about psychic phenomena to acquiesce and go with it.

She jutted her chin. "I'm not sure what you mean, Devorah."

"Well, let's just say that if there is a young man, there will be some short-term fulfillment to the relationship. However, I can't tell you that it will end well." The vision left me with more foreboding than my familiar neuroses usually provided.

"Why? How will it end…if there is such a relationship?"

"Remember that I can't tell you how to live your life, right? You choose what to do with any information I give you. I just get the feeling that this will cost you much more than pay dividends." Most of my clients responded to money references best.

"Okay, I'll take that under advisement. Tell me, that giant sword there, what does it mean?"

She was pointing at the Ace of Swords. It was placed, tellingly, in the future position, and it made me squirm in recognition. "Well, sometimes the swords are about intellect and communication. How we make our choices and how we rationalize them to ourselves and others." I was completely unclear how to convey the information to a woman who was making devastating choices for herself. I had to pause for a few moments and gather myself. The card was staring at me, daring me to reveal what I knew to be true about my client.

"Look, I have to go back to the young man. I know this is difficult, but I'm compelled to tell you what I'm learning from the cards." I wasn't ready to inform a stranger that I'd just had a vision of her having sex. Her face was frozen as she watched me. "There is some information about this young man that you need to know in order to continue with your… your friendship. You must learn more about him or this will probably end poorly." I hated giving my clients bad news, but this time it felt crucial to this woman's well-being.

I could tell she was a little deflated but unwilling to let go of whatever it was she was planning with the boy. The coy bend of her head informed me that she knew exactly who I was talking about, that she was deluding herself somehow and making the choice to continue.

"If this information about the young man is so important, Devorah, why don't you go and find it out yourself. Then you can call me and fill me in. In the meantime, I intend to trust my instincts."

I knew she was being facetious about me finding the information about this boy, but there was a sense of rightness about it. A mission. However, I didn't want to become involved with my clients and their misery.

I didn't know if I had caught a peek of the future or the past. Or even if it was just a ghost of my client's deepest wish. But the visions continued, not occasionally, but with every reading thereafter. Over the years, I came to realize my visions were not hallucinations but possible futures, likely to become certain if nobody intervened.

And the outcome of my first vision? The young man was a notorious, drug-addled teen actor. Six months after that reading, my predictably jilted client descended into acute depression and gun-blazing suicide.

The chilling suicide incident churned gnarling guilt that kept my stomach in a constant state of complaint. I had to ask myself some uncomfortable questions, and those questions led to an idea. If I could see what might happen in the future, could I do something to change it? Should I get involved?

So I started telling my clients what they could do to fix their situations. A breakup, maybe, or a threatened lawsuit. They were just suggestions, and my clients almost always swore they didn't have the courage to carry through the necessary steps to change their lives. A few times I was asked to write a breakup letter, and in each case, the letters I wrote worked. My clients emerged from their predicaments with fewer wounds than their readings had predicted.

So I started testing things. I would give clients a strong suggestion about how to handle a sticky situation that was bedeviling them. Then I'd follow up with them. Even if they carried out my suggestion to the letter, the results weren't satisfying, only half complete. However, if I carried out the suggestions myself, the results were exemplary. A client would win a lawsuit, get the dream job, obtain revenge. The measures I had to take were spelled out to me in the tarot cards through their images, numbers, and meanings.

It was as if some cosmic game had me as its only strategist and player. Why me, I wondered. Well, why not, I'd answer back. And would my clients pay me to alter the probable outcome as testified in their cards? Yes, they would. And they did, substantially.

Soon I was doing more than just reading tarot cards for clients. I was "reorganizing." I adore euphemisms. Words like "enhanced interrogation" or "reeducation" to describe torture are morbidly amusing to me. Reorganizing was an enhanced service for my clients, for an exponentially larger fee that varied depending upon difficulty of the assignment. I took steps to realign my clients' trajectories. I wrote authentic-appearing letters, impersonated attorneys, mildly threatened light blackmail, and posted convincing packages. Whatever it took to alter the likelihoods in my visions, my clients paid me to do it. Was it a little lawless? Yes. was anyone harmed? I'd like to think not, but I'm not sure. Was my work dangerous? I hoped not. Did I love it? I used to.

I was probably the best paid tarot reader on the planet. My name wasn't famous. No infomercials, websites, books, or sycophantic followers. My clients kept my name and contact information in strict confidence. There would be a month's worth of tabloid caterwauling if the paparazzi knew what I knew about each of my clients. A Hollywood or Washington D.C. psychotherapist had less career-killing information than I had. I was the uneasy carrier of secrets, and I performed the deeds that secrets are made of. I was the ultimate professional *kochleffl*, a mixing spoon, the meddler who fixed people's lives for a fee.

To protect myself as much as my clients, I kept no notes. No little black book. No diary for my tell-all memoir. I had a plain off-white business card with my work-dedicated cell number printed under my professional name, Devorah Rosten. My social friends believed my money came from a little light card reading and a giant trust fund. I figured "family money" would be generic enough to avoid scrutiny of Dev, the social animal. If, in the upscale clubs and cocktail parties I frequented, I crossed paths with one of my clients, I wrung my hands for a few minutes. But then I remembered that my clients thought I knew their dirty secrets. No client would dare break my cover. I knew too much.

I crept out of my fortified psychic compound to tell this story. I was obliged to go against all my personal and professional ethics to record one client's tale. She deserved to have the dangerous truth recorded somewhere, by another person, to keep her safe. I couldn't refuse Laura Bishop.

CHAPTER TWO

When I was thirteen, my aunt Ruthie gave me a pack of tarot cards for my bat mitzvah. For a few minutes, the gift pleased me because it was edgy, Aunt Ruthie's best quality. But I noticed our synagogue's cantor-with-the-stick-up-her-tuchas grimacing at the decidedly inappropriate gift for a devout young Jewish woman. A few days later, I nervously nudged the deck away into a bat mitzvah mementos box and forgot about it. For years.

I never was a mystic seeker or believer in the arcane. Quite the opposite, in fact. My mother raised me conventionally Jewish in a conservative synagogue in Boston. My sharp-tongued father, whose parents barely survived Auschwitz, was tepid about anything Jewish and refused to attend temple with my mother and me. He seemed to live on the edge of a precipice of doom, and, for him, public displays of Judaism were the prod that would topple him over the edge. On the other hand, he was fluent in Yiddish, as was my mother. Consequently, I grew up steeped in two languages.

Father died slowly, with ferocious, protesting fanfare, from cancer when I was twelve years old. He made clear in his final wishes that there were to be no Jewish or goyish rituals to mark his passage. My mother obeyed his last request probably to forestall any possibility that his ghost would return to kvetch at her one more time. Then she became doubly active in our synagogue community where, for the first time in years, she acquired comfort and friendship.

My spiritual search consisted of questioning whether "going kosher" would hamper my dating life. I decided it would make things more problematic with the shiksa girlfriends, so kosher was ruled out. I did, however, require a low wheat and dairy diet to help manage my chronic allergies.

I was a timorous hedonist looking for the next sensual experience while making sure I wasn't in danger or exposed to some errant noxious germ. The crystal visionaries of new-age doctrine bewildered me, and I often found opportunities to mock them and their followers. Then I had a simple dream.

I was sitting on a bale of hay at some sort of outdoor festival. A spread of tarot cards lay on the bale in front of me. I was bending intently over the cards, so much so that my usual tangle of black curls obscured a few of the cards. I saw my hand impatiently pull and hold the locks behind my neck. I could feel the prickling of straw through my lightweight cotton pants. I shifted to ease the tickling. On the other side of the card spread sat a rapt listener. Her mouth shaped in an astounded *O*, she believed every word I said. I looked at the cards and uttered to myself, "But I've never seen tarot cards before. In fact, I've never even seen a bale of hay before."

When I woke up, every second of that dream vignette was permanently scored in my brain. So I grabbed a chair, climbed into the rarely visited, spidery attic, and found the bat mitzvah memento box from twelve years earlier. Pushing aside mazel tov cards, petrified cake, and deflated balloons, I landed upon the still-shiny box of tarot cards. The box's plastic wrapper was never opened. I could feel Aunt Ruthie smiling all the way from Florida.

I was captured by the cards. They fascinated me and held me in a grip difficult to describe. But it was unbreakable. The symbols, each with several possible meanings, fanned before me were the book of life, the keys to knowledge beyond science.

I didn't have much money at the time, but what little I made teaching third grade at the Jewish day school, I spent on material about tarot. All kinds of books, pamphlets, software, anything pertaining to the cards, and I continued to collect for years.

My mother cheerfully enjoyed widowhood and devoted her free time to cajoling me into finding "a good Jewish girl with a respectable job." She would phone my hovel of a Seattle apartment from Boston and tell me where to find a proper girlfriend and a better-paying job she could be proud of. She didn't know I had found a Jewish love. Much of tarot cosmology is based on ancient Jewish Kabbalah.

"Mama, your kibitzing isn't helping. All good things happen in their time."

"Your aunt Ruthie calls every week and asks after you. What am I to tell her? She worries."

"Somehow, I think you're the worrier and Aunt Ruthie is just making polite conversation. If you want to worry about something, worry about this spot of eczema I'm growing below my left ear. It bothers me, and I wonder if it could develop into something worse."

"Dev-uh-lah, a little dry skin patch by your ear is not a sign of eczema or, God forbid, cancer. I don't know where you get this tendency to make every bodily tic into some horrible disease. You need a nice attentive girlfriend to take your mind

KRISTIN MARRA

off yourself. You two could find a good Jewish boy to donate his help and give me a few grandchildren and—"

"Enough, Mama, enough. I'll let you know when I fall in love, okay? Right now I'm sure this dry skin is eczema or maybe psoriasis. How do you tell the difference?"

I really didn't care about getting a girlfriend while I researched tarot. Oh, I dated, had sex, sent flowers, and batted my eyes with the best of them. I was complacent and smug that women found my yoga-sculpted physique irresistible. But a steady girlfriend would have distracted me from my real mission: to understand the cards. So I remained distractedly single, defying my mother's obsessive dreams of grandchildren and nursing my phobic obsession with physical symptoms.

For three years, I studied cards while sitting at my wobbly, chrome and Formica table in my cramped kitchen. It was the ancient symbols, their multiple meanings and their connection to something beyond me, beyond this physical realm that enthralled me. I came to understand metaphor and how each spread is a metaphor for the question at hand. And the metaphor came from somewhere else, an ethereal hand, writing a message in a universal language of symbols. Each card, its picture, number, or place in the spread held information.

I reasoned that tarot was a method to communicate with "the other side." A technology, if you will, but not a technology they study at MIT, as my mother would have reminded me had she known what I was doing. This was a technology made of seventy-eight cards, and these cards were phone lines to the keepers of infinite knowledge. By sitting with the images, information came to me, larger truths about life, about the connectedness of everything in the universe. I was on the edge of knowing all, each card a key to wisdom.

I felt wired into something far larger than the mundane

world around me. Some days, I'd reach such a deep, stimulating connection with universal truths that I'd have to run the few miles to my yoga instructor's studio, take a couple of grueling classes back-to-back, and run home, just to be able to function in the mundane world of grocery shopping and classroom lesson plans.

For months, I didn't tell anyone what I was doing. I was embarrassed about taking up something so *meshugana*, crazy, as card reading. Eventually, though, I couldn't *not* talk about it. The cards, their stories, were becoming a part of me, defining my experience. It was as if I'd learned another language and was translating all my experiences into my new symbolic vocabulary. My knowledge of Hebrew helped, along with my comfort with Jewish symbols. And I'm certain that during that time of personal awakening, my dairy allergy was a little better.

Eventually, an astonishing thing happened: when I talked about tarot to my friends, they wanted me to do a reading for them. Very few looked at me like I'd gone over sanity's precipice. More often, they looked at me like I'd know too much about them, but they couldn't resist asking for what I could find out from the cards. Reluctantly at first, I became a professional reader, but then I morphed into a darn good one after a few years. I made some money and decided to substitute teach instead of hold a full-time job. I finally stopped teaching altogether and moved into a bigger apartment.

After a few years of being an excellent, but normal, tarot reader, I had the experience with the female client, the boy, and the suicide. Consequently, I started helping clients redirect their trajectories, and I got rich doing so. I was discovered by the rich and famous, so my practice flourished with glitterati seeking my advice and interventions. It was also during that period that Laura Bishop came to see me that first time, and I started following her career.

Except for some chronic acid reflux, life was working out perfectly. Then things took a turn.

❖

I was reading for a client who planned to extort money out of her famous and wealthy stepfather. He had molested her when she was a girl. She wanted to make him pay for years of trauma. She sought guidance from the cards. It was one of the disquieting occasions when I felt tremendous empathy for a client and would feel guilty if I didn't help her somehow. I laid a standard Celtic Cross spread. It's a spread used to help clients know their current barriers, the past experiences that contribute to the present, and the future outlook if things don't change. The significator, the card that represents the client, turned up the High Priestess. But in this case, the austere card seemed all wrong for the complicated woman across from me. My deep instinct knew that card, the severe High Priestess, was for me.

I couldn't pull my eyes away from the frozen face on that card. Then my body was viciously suctioned through a funnel. There was a violent constriction around my head, a sensation as if my brains would spurt out my ears. The pain immediately disappeared and I found myself standing behind a small dais. I was facing the back of an elaborately crowned woman seated on a simple throne. She was looking at what resembled a giant green screen used for movie special effects. To my right towered a white marble pillar, and a black pillar stood to my left.

"Ah, finally, a human. It's been a while," said a dry,

papery voice. The woman in front of me was speaking. "No, this doesn't mean your client is going to become a queen, so you won't get richer from her. Quit the panic breathing and come around to face me, dunce. Then you'll know where you are and how unlucky you are."

Frightened and mystified by her awareness of me, I stepped off the dais and moved in front of the woman. My stomach bobbled its breakfast when I saw her. I covered my eyes and fought the nausea. Sinking to my knees, I whimpered, unwilling to dare another look. I was certain any shred of sanity I once blithely possessed had been abandoned to psychotic hallucinations. I worried if I'd finally reached my lifetime ceiling of Benadryl.

"Oh, gather yourself, pathetic child. You haven't taken leave of your senses. You won't come to harm here. As for your fate in your…realm, I can't be so optimistic. Now look at me and tell me what you see. Your well-being depends upon you accepting what is happening. Don't grovel. Just look."

Every molecule within me knew that if I looked, my life would alter forever. And it was such a nice little life too. On my knees, my eyes covered, I tried to weigh the ramifications. Unable to muster anything resembling lucidity, I looked.

Before me, on a stone throne, sat an elongated, chisel-featured woman wearing an absurd crown made of two half-moons with an orb between them. Her blue cape covered most of the red dress that was decorated by a simple wooden crucifix hanging from a chain that encircled her neck. In her lap, she loosely held a worn, leather-bound Torah. One foot reached from beneath her robes and idly rocked a crescent moon back and forth. It was the only movement she made. The moon squeaked like the lid of a Styrofoam cooler as it rocked against the floor.

But what got me were her eyes. They were like marbles, unnatural as the glass eyes one sees in taxidermy. They didn't move to track me, but I knew she saw me. It was as if whoever inhabited that form was hiding inside it, using it as a costume, using those eyes as peepholes to spy on me.

Visions of the future were one thing; this was a whole other psychic experience I'd never heard of.

"Oh, shit."

"An intellectual, I see. Formidable command of the language." The High Priestess of Tarot, in the flesh, sort of, was looking at me like I was something stuck under a lunch counter. "Well, tell me where you are," she demanded.

"I…I'm with you."

"They've sent me a brilliant one. Who am I? Say it."

"The Priestess…the High Priestess." The words stuck to my tongue. Denial riding me fast and hard.

"Thank you for not using that dreadful moniker, 'the Papess.' So seventeenth century, wouldn't you say? Or maybe more twenty-first century gynecologic." A sandpaper chuckle.

"Sure. It…ah…it, the Papess, doesn't cover who you are, in my opinion."

"Or *what* I am, for that matter. But all that is for a later discussion, if I'm in the mood. You're here for your purpose… your destiny, if you want to get mawkish and dramatic about it."

"This is real? Not a hallucination, opium dream, Benadryl overdose?"

"Ah, a jester too. More fitting. If you want this to be any of those things, I can help."

Her faced morphed into a pea-green, red-eyed horse head and then morphed back to her face.

"Don't do that!" I covered my eyes again.

She laughed a bristly, grating wheeze. No smile. "You'd be fun to toy with if you weren't needed, dolt. But it's fallen upon me to educate you and make you ready for the Malignity."

"The Malignity?"

"Now I'm training a parrot. Is this the best we could get? They told me you had a prodigious mind."

"Hey, I'm starting to resent the way you speak to me. How should I know why I'm here, or even how I got here? This isn't my choice." I stood now, halfheartedly ready to defend myself.

"Sorry, but you made this choice the day you dared dabble in the forces behind tarot or those other lamentable cosmologies. You know as well as I that you are playing with universal forces. Seeing the future, then working to change it. What did you think you were doing? You've manipulated us long enough. Now we will manipulate you."

"Manipulate me how? And what's this 'Malignity'?" Nothing was sitting well on my anxious belly, especially words that reminded me of a dreaded disease.

"It's no disease." Great, she could read my thoughts. "You may view it as a pestilence in your part of the cosmos. A persistent force of energy readying itself to destroy your current world and realign the powers that control. Others call the Malignity necessary."

"And I should care because…"

"Let me name a few times when the Malignity has strengthened. Shall I mention Pope Innocent III's Crusade in France, or any of the other Crusades?"

"They killed blameless people?"

"Millions. I'll name something more modern and delectable for the historically illiterate. Europe during the first half of the twentieth century and the mechanization of murder by the Nazis. Or let's try a more localized current affair: North Korea."

"Are you saying some sort of totalitarianism is coming? Where? How?" We Jews get jumpy at the thought of dictatorial political systems. By that point in our history, distrust of dictators was probably genetically encoded into my people.

I noticed she had barely moved during our entire encounter. In fact, just her mouth seemed to move, and the incessant foot that rocked the moon crest on the floor. All else was still and quiet. Her eyes caught the light like glass. Her skin resembled the fleshy tone common to store mannequins.

She noticed my noticing her lack of movement and flicked her wrist stiffly. A wave of revulsion hit when I saw she had no fingernails, just tapered ends, like new candle tips.

"The Malignity, it's always here, kept at bay, but somtimes it grows until meddlers step in. You are a meddler, but a meddler with ambiguous intentions: either you want money or to assuage your guilt. Perfect. Or a possible problem. But this time, we chose you as our human champion. We've learned that using armies is counter-productive. Enjoyable to watch, but too much destruction, repair, and wasted time. One meddler can often quietly accomplish our goals without the bloody fanfare we loved in the past."

I started glancing around for an escape. There was no door, no window, not even a skylight. "I don't remember interviewing for the position of…of…whatever you're looking for." I wanted to look behind the tapestry framing her, the one covered with stylized pomegranates.

"You cannot leave without my permission. Cease searching for an exit."

"What about my client? She's waiting for me."

The High Priestess's unsettling hand moved stiffly again,

lifting slightly as if to make grudging acknowledgment. "Her ridiculous situation is resolved in her favor. She thinks you are in a trance. When you 'wake up,' you can inform her."

"What's this 'education' you're talking about? What am I supposed to do? I'm not a soldier, spy, or crime fighter, you know. And I have a bad tennis elbow." I kneaded my left elbow.

Again, that sandy laugh and it raised the hair on my arms. "We believe in what you humans call on-the-job training. We will contact you at the appropriate hour. Remember, we have a different experience of time in this realm."

"Who's 'we'?"

"Another time. I grow weary of you. Crawl behind me and touch the white pillar, dunderhead."

"If you think I'm going to work for someone who treats me like—" Before taking a step, I was hurled against the pillar. By what, I couldn't say. The High Priestess hadn't moved. I opened my eyes while rubbing my bashed forehead.

"Hey, why'd you—" I looked up at my client sitting across the table staring at me, her mouth slightly ajar. I was back to normalcy.

I did what the High Priestess ordered and told the client her problem was solved. She went away perplexed but happy.

That evening the same client called to inform me her stepfather had died that very day of a brain aneurism. He left every dime of his money to her. Instead of being happy for her, I was so agitated that I had to double my dosage of sleeping herbs.

Chapter Three

For a while after meeting the High Priestess, life went on as usual. I discovered more refined ways of altering the probable future. In truth, I worked on being less intrusive. I started to worry that my methods had further-ranging effects than I'd previously believed. I think it was the High Priestess calling me a "meddler" that got my attention. I became suspicious that the reason only my personal intervention ever drew satisfactory results was because the High Priestess was the source of my abilities.

So I took to studying my clients' circumstances more closely. If necessary, I'd call on my sadistic hacker genius, Fitch. She could go where no hacker had ever gone before. She could uncover unsavory secrets (porn addiction, mistresses, embezzlement) about someone who was tormenting a client and pass the information on to me without questioning why I wanted it. Instead of issuing threats that smelled of extortion, I'd send an anonymous note hinting that a slight change in behavior toward my client could possibly result in said secret not being revealed. Repeat if necessary. Not as swift in results, sometimes, or as thrilling, but more mature. My fees stayed the same, however.

Months after that excursion to the High Priestess's little

room, I was reading cards for Hollywood's current tabloid starlet. We were focused on a secret child she had at age fifteen. The child was currently being cared for by an aunt who had designs on breaking the starlet's confidentiality unless a large financial compensation was supplied. A typical sort of hot seat my clients tended to occupy.

We were meeting in a luxury suite at a hotel in downtown Seattle. Outside, over the balcony, the Bainbridge ferry lumbered across the Puget Sound and the Olympic Mountains scribbled in the far horizon. One of those glorious days that belies Seattle's reputation as a rain capital.

The opulence of the suite where we sat had become mundane to me. My clients always wanted to meet in some lavish, yet private venue. I would have preferred a leaky tent in the wilderness for a change of pace, as long as I didn't have to spend the night. In this case, I was experiencing some empathy for my client and anger at the blackmailing aunt. I simmered at the inhumanity of holding an innocent child hostage.

Another Celtic Cross spread in front of me and, once again, I turned over the High Priestess. Just as I realized I hadn't seen the card in several readings, the meat grinder pressure wrapped my head and I was thrown into the black pillar that stood behind the High Priestess. Sprawled on my back, arms outstretched, I glared at the back of her throne.

"Could this be a more gentle process?" I was suffering from that particular hammer of anger I felt whenever I bashed my head into a rock-solid object.

"Soldiers don't whine. They rise and advance." The derisive sandpaper voice came from the front of the chair.

"Soldier? Advance? You sound like I'm marching into battle."

"Yes, that could suffice as a training ground, but it

wouldn't elicit the special conceptual skills needed for your mission."

"Look, I'm not cut out for 'missions.' I'm just a card reader with a specialty." I walked around the throne to look at the High Priestess for the second time. This time her eyes followed me, and her severe mouth twitched into a condescending sneer that she might have thought was a smile. I studied her for a long moment. A chill rocked me when I realized she didn't breathe.

"And I have no heartbeat. Organics are necessary in your realm, but they're decoration here. Little niceties strung here and there to make the occasional human visitor more... functional."

"So are you always reading my mind? Or do you have some privacy ethics?"

A scratching chuckle erupted from her. "Read your mind? Why indulge in such a dreary pastime? Your thoughts blare out of that humanly appealing visage of yours." She considered me for long moments until I felt like a specimen. My feelings were corroborated when she said, "Yes, you'll do, but just barely." She lifted her left arm and beckoned me closer.

"Come closer, Devorah Rosten. We have run out of time." She kept my eyes captive, and I found myself kneeling on the dais in front of her. "Your mission starts now."

Her icy finger tapped the place between my eyebrows, and I closed my eyes in spontaneous protection.

When I opened them again, I wasn't sitting in front of my client. I wasn't looking at the unnerving High Priestess. I was somewhere altogether different.

I scrambled to my feet, alarmed. My Tony Lama boots were sinking into soft dirt, so it took a moment to right myself. The sky was pallid turquoise and held no clouds. The sun was hot but queerly disc-like, as if an overheated dinner plate had been hung for warmth. It was doing a great job because sweat was tickling my back and forehead.

I was standing in the middle of a vast plowed field. The brown furrows stretched so far to my right and left they appeared endless. In front of me was a large, leafy tree overhanging an old-fashioned well, the kind with a bucket and rope. It was the same kind of well found in tarot cards. It usually meant delving into the deep unconscious to find hidden truths. "Let's hope there are some truths around here because I could use some answers," I said.

The heat from the weird sun was burning through the shirt on my back. To gain shade, I trundled toward the tree, struggling with the unstable dirt underneath my feet. "Plowed fields," I said to myself, "symbolizing the laying of groundwork for an arduous project. Oy."

Before I could reach the tree, I heard rhythmic clumping growing louder as it neared. Swirling and stumbling around, I gasped as a large white horse closed the distance between us. Sitting atop the charger was an honest-to-goodness knight in glinting medieval armor. He was bearing down on me, viciously swinging the largest sword imaginable. When it was clear he wasn't going to stop, I tried to run, but the soft dirt gave way beneath my feet.

The hooves drummed danger. In what seemed like hours, I made it to the well. I glanced up to find the knight upon me, then grabbed the bucket rope and slid over the edge. A layer of skin scraped onto the rope when it jerked and stopped unspooling from above. My screams echoed off the rock sides of the shaft. I thrust my feet out and pushed my back into the rock wall, struggling for stability.

"That was unwise, pretty damsel." In the circle of light

above, I could see the now helmetless head of the large man. His burnished hair draped the sides of his boxy chin. "All I need to do is sever the rope, and you will spend the rest of your days at the bottom."

"Who are you?" My voice was squeaking and would have been comical were I not in terrible pain and mortal fear.

"Ah, now that is a tale not for your ears at this time." He was almost barking his laugh. "You are a pretty raven-haired damsel. And I like the greenish color of your eyes. I will let you live today." He emitted an odd practiced giggle. "Hold tight. I will pull you out. Just keep in mind I am not always a rescuer of damsels."

"I'm definitely not a damsel." I grunted when he dragged me over the jagged edge of the well and dropped me on the ground.

"So you say. It will take some time for you to prove that if your plunge into the well is any indication." He spoke in such formal English that it sounded like he was reading his lines from a script.

"Please tell me who you are," I said as I stared at my bloody, stinging palms.

"For now, I am your…let us say, builder or trainer."

"I already have a personal trainer at my gym. She's better looking than you. And I'm not learning to ride a horse or swing a giant sword. Do you have something to wrap around my hands? They could get infected, you know."

He pulled out a long white kerchief, tossed it to me, and said, "No swords. No horses. But this realm"—he looked around the vast fields—"is your learning ground. You need to know its rules, its limitations, and its meaning. It is admirable work, is it not? I call it 'the Theater.'" He studied me for several moments, paying closest attention to my hair. "That is fascinating hair, damsel. All those stretched curls will be interesting to reproduce sometime. I venture to guess that humans find you attractive, like I do."

"Why me? Why am I here?" I wrapped the kerchief around my left hand since it appeared to have received the worst punishment.

"Because you can get here. And because you are of the meddler line, chosen by the Lady. We members of the House of Coyne are her allies and, when it suits us, her servants."

"Line?" I looked up from blowing on my right palm. That's when I spied the circle on the front of his tunic. Within the embroidered circle was a pentacle, a five-point star. I was looking at tarot's Knight of Pentacles.

"Your education will begin now. Prepare yourself, damsel, and look there." He pointed toward the field. Kneeling near us was a woman, blond, her head bent over her chest as if she were grieving. Nine swords riddled the ground around her, a reminder of the card that symbolized grief.

"Who is she?" I asked. At the sound of my voice, she lifted her head and looked at me. I was shackled and conscripted by those brown eyes exuding compassion, forgiving me all my foibles and sins. This was a woman who knew how to love. It was Laura Bishop. I tried to step toward her but couldn't move.

"Why you?" I said. She couldn't hear me. It was like she was a kind of projection, not a real person. The image of her faded.

"Damsel, from now on, nothing is coincidence," the knight said. "Indeed, it never was."

The Knight of Pentacles's finger touched my forehead, and I was looking at my distraught client in the sumptuous Seattle hotel room. I assured her that the situation would resolve itself soon. She went away satisfied. I believed the High Priestess would fix things for her. I just didn't know how and knew it didn't matter.

The bloody scrapes on my hands had disappeared, but the pain still burned. I pressed my palms onto my thighs. There was a small wet bar in the room, and I decided some seltzer water would help my clawing stomach.

I stood at the window, gazed down to the glistening wet Seattle street, and remembered watching Laura Bishop walk away from the same building so many years ago. My reverie was interrupted by a caravan of cars pulling up in front of the hotel. One of the cars was a large limousine. Before the doors of the limo were opened, the other cars in the caravan spilled out a muscle brigade of bodyguards. They appeared to be directed by one particular brute with a bald head. He seemed familiar, but it was difficult to recognize distinguishing features from so far above.

Then the limousines opened, and I forgot Mr. Gym Rat. It wasn't a challenge to recognize who emerged. I could see his distinctive pompadour, the silver sideburns accentuated his blacktop hair. I didn't need to be down there to know he sported a smug half grin. I resisted pulling the window open to toss my pitiful few drops of seltzer water on his head.

"Jerry Greenfield. Oy, what a *trombenik.*" A blowhard phony is what he was. A so-called religious man who had designs on transforming the country into a theocracy. He wanted the Constitution amended to make his religion the mandate of the state. His flagrant demonization of gay people, unmarried mothers, socialists, and immigrants won him many followers from the frightened masses. They needed scapegoats for their woes, and Jerry Greenfield was supplying them. He claimed he supported Jews, but I knew Jews would be next on his list if his current list of "evil souls bred of Satan" lost their scare punch. As a gay person, I was already his followers' nightmare. It was only a matter of time before they fell upon the Jews. They always had before in history; no reason things should change.

"What's he doing in Seattle?" I wondered aloud. Then I remembered his wife was in town campaigning. Elizabeth Stratton, U.S. senator, was Jerry Greenfield's wife and colleague in creating mayhem. Formerly a Seattle attorney, Washington state's Senator Stratton was now running a campaign to gain the nomination for president of the United States, an odious outcome if there ever was one.

No sooner had I thought of Elizabeth Stratton than she emerged from the limo surrounded by more enormous, buzz-cut bodyguards. Her long salt-and-pepper hair was perfectly tended into a chignon, and I could make out her aristocratic profile. Her charisma enveloped her like a cloud of strong perfume. Charisma and righteous certitude was what she used to spread misinformation and lies to her adoring fans. She wasn't a politician anymore. She was a personality who controlled the thinking of millions of deluded people who were hungry for a leader, a leader who gave voice to their deepest hate and dread.

I was sickened when I turned away from the window. Even being in the same building with those two parasites disrupted my sensibilities. Something jangled my memory, but it was beyond my grasp. What was I missing about Stratton? There was a connection, a feeling, but I couldn't grasp it. I repeated what the Knight of Pentacles had said to me: "Damsel, from now on, nothing is coincidence. Indeed, nothing ever was."

❖

After spotting Jerry Greenfield and Elizabeth Stratton, I returned to my condo a few blocks north of the hotel. I needed to contemplate the encounter with the Knight of Pentacles, whom I cheekily renamed Pento. I resolved to avoid doing readings for a few weeks. This required rescheduling some important and pissed-off clients. But I was afraid of another surprise toss into the Theater. I wanted to see if there was a way, on my side of reality, to control my access to the High Priestess and Pento.

I also needed time to reflect on what I'd learned about the dimension, for lack of a better noun, I'd visited. The High Priestess and Pento had a disturbing way of reminding me of a little book I once read about a girl who enters a land where all the inhabitants have buttons sewn on their faces to replace their eyes. Shocking. Unnatural.

The two human-like characters and the horse I'd met in that other world didn't breathe, and I knew they didn't sport beating hearts or, probably, growing hair. And the High Priestess's lack of fingernails roiled my always-sensitive stomach. The Priestess, Pento, the horse, and the landscape were manufactured somehow. Did that make them my hallucination?

And what about the woman, Laura Bishop, the one whose eyes reached to me and cradled something inside me that was deeply sad? Except online and in newspapers, I hadn't seen her in years, since the reading when I warned her she was in danger.

What was happening? It appeared I was psychically batted between demeaning interviews with the High Priestess, encounters with Pento, plus Laura Bishop and her heartrending eyes.

From what I could fathom, I was having three separate paranormal or, worse, psychotic experiences. I was catching glimpses of my clients' futures, getting humiliated in the High Priestess's barren throne room, and diving down wells in some fabricated world. Were these really separate experiences? Did they have some cosmic relationship? Was I losing my mind? It was time to retreat.

❖

Northwest of Seattle's cityscape floats a paradise called the San Juan Islands. Several years ago, I bought twelve acres of pristine waterfront land on Lopez Island, the southernmost island in the archipelago. On that wooded property, overlooking Hunter Bay, I built the home of my acquisitive dreams. A client who was a well-known architect bartered his original design for ten readings. It was worth every minute of discussing his annoying fetish for wearing diapers and how to keep his church brethren from finding out.

The house took two years to build, due to the special shipments and imports involved when creating a magnificent structure on an island. I was mistress of a sumptuous 4,500 square foot lookout over the bay. The house was equipped with a high-tech air purification system and state-of-the-art security system. The library contained the most extensive collection of tarot print material anywhere in the world. My bedroom jutted over the cliff and supplied a 180 degree view of the water while I lay in bed and read.

The house was my sanctuary. I named it Tranquility. Tranquility was the emotion I always felt when I pondered the Star, the number seventeen of the major arcana of the tarot. The card depicted a serene woman, often naked, taking water from a lake and pouring it both onto the land and back into the lake. She surrounded herself in beauty and the stars she gazed at. She symbolized, to me, the boundless beauty in the universe, ever renewing. And the card's number seventeen, a prime number, undisturbed by numerous factors. I even had an artist create a large porcelain floor tile that depicted the woman from the Star card and had the tile set in the cement on my front porch at Tranquility. It served as a reminder for why I had built the house.

I always went to Tranquility to escape the disturbing elements of my oddball existence.

So the Theater experience prompted me to temporarily close my more modest condo in downtown Seattle and sequester myself at Tranquility. My goal was to develop some control over the dismaying teleportation I was experiencing. Shifting into other worlds with clients watching was not a sound business plan.

I made my library at Tranquility the center of operations. It was the most tarot-centered room probably in the world. It contained thousands of volumes, pamphlets, and folios about tarot and related topics. I also had collected antique arcane objects from the systems of Wicca and Kabbalah. These were stored in temperature-controlled glass cases. Knives, chalices, crystals, and other items were displayed in the cases. My collection also consisted of hundreds of different tarot decks, many were centuries old and hand painted. I was a compulsive collector of items from the mystery traditions. The collective energy of the items in my library infused me with a sense of wonder and power.

After I settled into Tranquility, unpacking and stocking groceries, I went to my library to begin the research. I spread my cards on the big oak worktable located in the center of the room. I readied myself to meet my buddies—the High Priestess, Pento, and, my real hope, Laura Bishop.

The first angle of attack was to isolate the trigger that pulled me into the Theater. I assumed it had to rest somewhere in the cards, probably with the High Priestess card or the Knight of Pentacles. Focusing, I stared into both cards, first individually, then as a pair. Nothing. I turned them at odd angles, looked at them reversed, made faces at them. I even tried intoning Hebrew prayers over them. Still nothing.

For days, I gazed at cards, in hundreds of configurations, in futile attempts to shoot myself into Pento's Theater. At one point, I resorted to dancing around the table singing "Bohemian Rhapsody." I had the uneasy feeling the High Priestess was laughing at my lamentable efforts. I spent hours scrutinizing arcane tarot books, yellowed monographs, and musty folios, praying for a clue. I studied the symbols, hoping exposure to one of them would spark something. But I had to give up that particular avenue since the tarot is an extensive, seemingly bottomless stew of symbols. It would take years to isolate the particular trigger symbol if there were one. And I wasn't sure there was a trigger located in the cards.

As a reader, I had one odd disability. I couldn't remember the exact card spread for any particular client. The spread dissolved from my gray matter the minute the client left my presence. My memory glitch made it impossible for me to recreate the spreads that sent me into the Theater.

I could remember the gist of the reading, the clients' stories, but the specific cards? Never.

After a week of hair-pulling frustration, I gave up. I was sick of looking at the damn things anyway. I was grateful I hadn't scheduled another reading for a few more weeks. The cards were smirking at me.

CHAPTER FOUR

Battering winter rain filled the house with incessant drumming, infusing the atmosphere with that distinctly Pacific Northwest gloom, a comfort for the souls of those who love living there. It had been seven days since I last looked at cards. The break was welcome, but I was beginning to feel explosive with frustrated anticipation.

The causes of my anxiety, I decided, were a lazy Susan of choices. I chalked it up to cabin fever, my daily walks curtailed by rain, no sex in weeks, and any other plausible but inaccurate excuse. I was afraid of my next trip to the High Priestess. Since I hadn't discerned the trigger into the Theater, I couldn't control it. If I couldn't control it, I was frightened. The memory of hanging in that well with Pento peering down at me produced a sheen of sweat on my brow.

In my futile search for the trigger to the High Priestess's dais, I hadn't reproduced the one thing that was consistent with all the other times I'd been shot into the other world: another person, a client, was present. Did I need a witness? Was that other person a part of the portal?

❖

"Hey, Fitch, got time for a weird-fest?"

"And you're choosing me because?" I could hear her amusement through the dicey cellular connection between the stormy island and Seattle.

"Because you have the most out-of-the-box mind I know, and I need your take on things. Come out to Lopez and work with me for a few days."

"Can I bring a 'helper' with me? You know, for relaxation, since you've made it so clear you're not my type of relaxation material."

"Any other time I'd say it's okay, twisted sister, but this time allows no distractions and probably little relaxation. You'll be, um, working." The last thing I needed was one of Fitch's slaves screaming and gasping while I was focusing on matters of the cosmos.

"Working? And my compensation would be what?"

"Besides availing yourself to my disgustingly overpriced wine cellar, you can name it, just no 'tie me up, tie me down' festivities with yours truly involved. Readings, money, a new slave…those kinds of things."

"How can I say no? My mind reels at the possibilities. Okay, I'll empty the slaves from my dungeon, pack up, and be out by…how about tomorrow evening?"

"Perfect. Oh, and bring some video equipment, would you?"

❖

Fitch and I had met several years previously when she hired me for a tarot reading. My vision revealed one of her technology clients trying to massacre her with a jaw-droppingly large assault weapon. He was convinced Fitch knew his filthy secrets of which, at the time of the reading, Fitch was ignorant.

"I have no idea what this dude is hiding. He just hired me to develop a more efficient tech network between dozens of his real estate offices." Fitch was pressing her hands on the table, her pinched mouth expressing far more anger than fear.

"How are your hacker skills?" An idea was formulating and she was swift in catching my meaning.

"I'm the best. It's what I do. Shall I start digging?" It was the first time I'd seen the grin of a sadist in action. It convinced me that, while she was darkly gorgeous, Fitch and I would never spend time tickling each other's fancy. She was dangerous, but she could be useful.

My intuition was that the man who would want to murder Fitch was hiding something sexual. He was financially successful and, we learned, married with children. Secrets of men like him usually consisted of some seedy sexual activity.

Fitch was at her computer less than an hour before she uncovered her prospective murderer's predilection for pedophilia. He had it all: videos, magazine subscriptions, websites, and a pimp who would text him via his phone when there were child sex orgies in Seattle and the cost of admission to the maggot-fest. There were even videos of him molesting small children, and he had stupidly stored them on his office computer.

"Okay, Rosten, pay dirt," she said over the phone and told me what she had found. "What should I do next? Kidnap and torture? I can do that."

A situation like that was a little tricky. On the one hand, we wanted him to back off Fitch, but on the other hand, we didn't want to blackmail him and cause him to come after her with that giant gun. "None of your overt remedies will work here. He's armed and may have friends. Can you send all those files anywhere, without them being traced back to you?"

"Child's play, Rosten. Where should they go for maximum effect?"

I had to think about that. The man's activities were illegal, so sending the files to the police vice division had to be included. But just for good measure, we sent the files to all his office managers, his wife, and just for entertainment, his minister.

He went to jail so quickly, it barely made a stir in the media. His wife, apparently not so attached to him as he thought, took over the real estate agencies and made them even more successful. We had no idea what the minister did with the files. Some things are best left a mystery.

After our joint adventure, I convinced Fitch that her skills would help me with my work. Fitch was a born snoop. I realized she could dig up more sensitive information than Homeland Security. A wealthy former tech guru, Fitch worked alone in her ultra-secure office in her waterfront home on Mercer Island, an upscale bedroom community of Seattle. She would be a perfect partner.

She was also a rampant hedonist and far more into BDSM than I was willing to contemplate, but she was loyal to me and completely closed-mouth. I had no idea who else Fitch scrounged information for. But I do know I paid scads of money for her services. Already rich, she loved the information more than she wanted the money.

❖

Harsh droplights illuminated my worktable in the library at Tranquility. The colors on the cards were running together in my exhausted vision. One video camera bore in on my face while another recorded each card spread. Fitch was stepping over cords and around video equipment in an effort to keep the cameras in focus and on target.

"Dev, can we stop now. Just for an hour? I'm hungry and need some exercise."

"And what would you do if one of your slaves asked you that question? C'mon, Fitch, just a few more card spreads. We have to hit it sometime."

"Hell, I'm still not sure what you mean when you say 'it.' Will you levitate? Fall into some kind of fit? Speak in tongues?" Fitch was fiddling with her video equipment while she kvetched. She had every right to complain. Even her black leather pants appeared baggy and wilted. We'd been at it for several hours. I was laying random spreads and waiting to see what happened. Fitch ran the cameras attempting to capture a clue as to what sent me to the High Priestess and the Theater.

"I'm not sure what I do when it happens. But I do know the clients who witnessed my shifting hardly knew what was happening. So my guess is you're going to have to wait until I come back around and tell you where I went. Then we can discuss your observations and replay the videos."

"Okay, a few more times, then I want to look at your wine cellar. You gotta keep the help happy."

We did six more spreads. My wrists were aching, and my hands started tingling from the countless times I had shuffled the deck that day. Leaving the last spread on the table, I was the one to start complaining. Well, more like whining.

"This isn't working, and my sinuses need flushing. I feel responsible for calling you out here, making you take a ferry, brave the rain, the roads, and all for nothing. And who knows, maybe I'm just a victim of some sort of vivid psychotic hallucinations."

"Hey, if it were anyone else, Dev, I'd think you might

be right about hallucinations. But not you. You're wrapped as tightly as anyone I know. Except for a little hypersensitivity to physical twitches, there are no loose bits rattling around inside your particularly gorgeous head. Go get a bottle of some great cabernet, a couple glasses, and let's kick this situation around a little more before we spread those fuckin' cards again."

I resented her swearing about my cards, but didn't feel it proper to chastise her. While I was pouring the fragrant red wine, we resumed our discussion.

Fitch was twirling her wine and sticking her nose into the glass to capture the wine's bouquet. Without looking up, she said, "This tarot thing, explain to me exactly what happens, and give me all the details."

As I did so, Fitch listened closely, asked clarifying questions and finally backtracked to the term "Malignity."

"So repeat again what times in history this High Priestess said were malignant times."

"The Crusades. I knew they were bad, but just a few days ago, I did some detailed research on them. Talk about a whitewashed piece of shameful history. The Church tricked thousands of ignorant men, women, and even children into slaughtering Muslims, Jews, or even more dismaying, their own people. 'Heretics,' they called them. A whole section of France was wiped out, including old people and children. Jews and Muslims were not people, just vermin to be exterminated. The soldiers believed it was for Christ, and their murderous behavior would get them into heaven. In reality, the pope and his henchmen just wanted to acquire and consolidate more power."

As I related what I knew about the Crusades, I could feel my indignation blossom. Then I got to the story of the Children's Crusade, a particularly evil part of the history, and my hands clamped as I stared at the forgotten tarot spread still on the table. I was bubbling with the desire to smash a medieval pope in the face. Then everything around me closed in. My head constricted and I squeezed my eyes shut. I felt forced through an exploding cannon. When I opened my eyes, I was staring into two horse nostrils.

The nostrils didn't move, didn't snuffle. The nostrils were not breathing.

"Where's the High Priestess?" I asked.

"She sent me instead. Have you imbibed in alcohol?" The Knight of Pentacles's helmeted head leaned around the lifeless horse muzzle. "I would like to taste alcohol. Humans seem so charmed by it. But since I cannot taste, sometime I will ask you to describe it to me."

"How can you tell I've been drinking? Do I smell? You couldn't smell a dead fish if it were rubbed on your upper lip."

"True, but you have red circles on your cheeks, and your eyes are not focused. I do not think you are ready for training in the Theater. The Lady did say you are not the most disciplined candidate to fight the Malignity."

"Look, I've just had a few sips. You try being forced through a psychic birth canal every time we meet, and I'll bet you'd look drunk too."

"Oh, is it painful to make the transition? I wondered. Hmm, well, nothing to be done about it. Let us just view it as part of your training since you will have to do it many times before this is over."

"'Before this is over.' 'The Malignity.' Oh crap."

"I did not say 'Oh crap.'"

"Ya know, Pento, this is going to be an interesting relationship."

"Pento?"

"Never mind. Just tell me what we do next."

"Certainly. That is why we are here. I am supposed to tell you the rules of engagement in this realm. We have constructed it for human purposes, but we cannot make it just like yours. We do not have perfect sensory information to do so."

"You've constructed all this?" I glanced around seeing the same plowed field, the odious water well I knew intimately, the tree, and the odd washed out blue sky.

"It is a world you know well. The world you see on your cards. This is where you will witness the malign force. It is the arena we have agreed upon for this particular battle in the eternal war. It is the Theater." He thrust out his chest and placed his fisted hands on his armor-protected waist.

"Eternal war? But you folks don't understand. I'm no fighter. I've never fought anybody, only manipulated lives. Changed the course of things, if you will."

"Which makes you perfect for the coming clash. Their champion wields the same weapons, but he is a determined adversary."

"He?"

"You will meet him soon in your realm, but he has a woman for a shield. You may not recognize him at first, as he may not recognize you. But when you finally meet, you will both be armed with a cause."

"You do realize that none of this makes much sense to me. How do I know I'm not suffering from some acute psychotic episode here? Maybe you're just a figment of my chemically imbalanced brain."

I looked into the unnaturally beaming sun and this time silently likened it to a bright flashlight, not a ball of burning gas hovering at the center of the solar system. The plowed dirt under my feet looked real, but when I bent to grab a handful, it felt more like pulverized packing material. In fact, little bits of it were sticking to my cross trainers, just like bits of Styrofoam do when they have a slight electrical charge. I didn't like it.

Pento must have seen my distaste. "Is the soil not to your liking? We have limits on what we can use to construct battle arenas. We have constructed a tarot world that will look somewhat like your world but does not bear close inspection if you are looking for accurate duplication. But we have had to do this before, construct Theaters for battle."

"Who usually wins the battles?"

Pento took a deep sigh. "Sometimes we win, and sometimes they win."

"Will you be explaining who 'we' and 'they' are? And what does winning look like?"

Pento opened his mouth to answer when a deafening crash made me wince and duck my head. When I looked up, Pento and the plowed field had been replaced by Fitch standing in my library bending over a toppled reading lamp.

"Damn, I hope this lamp wasn't valuable. I just tripped over the cord."

"Fitch, your timing sucks."

❖

Exhausted from my trip to the Theater, I told Fitch we could take a break and get something to eat. She was full of questions, but I couldn't talk about what happened. How could I tell anyone, even an aficionado of the twisted like Fitch, that I was either having outrageous psychic experiences or needed commitment to a psych ward?

I asked Fitch to make a few copies of me "in trance"

so that I'd have ample record of my corporeal body during the experience. I intended to study the recording to find the trigger, but I wanted to do it alone. I would have to wait a few days, however, because Fitch actually seemed worried about me and showed a rarely seen solicitous side of her personality. Since I wasn't her slave, I guessed she could afford to drop her dominatrix demeanor and show some caring for a friend. She even took off the exorbitantly priced leather pants, donned some well-worn jeans, and combed the spikes out of her black hair. She looked positively cute. For a few minutes, I considered inviting her to my bed, but after tracing the possible outcomes of such a folly, I discarded the idea.

"'Sin is sweet in the beginning but bitter in the end,'" I said half to myself.

"What?"

"Oh, nothing, just a little Talmudic wisdom. It keeps me above water."

"Okay, Dev, whatever it takes."

"You don't have to stay, you know, Fitch. I have the recording I need and am paying you handsomely for."

"Hell, you know money isn't my motivation. You're kinda my friend. I think I'll just hang out for a day or two and keep an eye on things. Can we get take-out somewhere around here?"

I was about to answer when an unfamiliar tinkling sound interrupted us. It was my doorbell.

"Wow, I hardly ever hear that. Wait in the kitchen, Fitch, just in case it's one of my clients. Though finding me out here…"

Another tinkle and Fitch swore she would stay in the kitchen while I went to the front door, another thing I rarely used since I always came through the garage. The door was stuck, warped from being rain soaked and not opened often.

I gave it several sharp jerks, and finally wrenched it open, flinging it back against the wall.

"Sorry about that. The builder warned me a wooden door would stick, but I had to ignore him and—"

The figure in front of me was hooded in a coat of pricey lamb's wool. When she pulled the hood off, I first saw how severely her hair was pulled into a bun. Her glasses reflected the porch light, disguising her eyes. She had a regal bearing but was trying to disguise herself, if not from me, from people on the road or passersby. Since the road was fifty yards away, obscured by trees, I knew her manner of caution was habit born of necessity.

"Are you Devorah Rosten?"

"Definitely. How did you find this place? I try to keep it from general knowledge."

"I'm sure I don't have to tell you how easy information is to obtain, Ms. Rosten."

Then I recognized her. The candidate. *The* candidate. Senator Elizabeth Stratton, soon to be nominated by the far right for president of the United States. Reverend Jerry Greenfield's wife. I wasn't happy.

"I won't pretend I don't know who you are, Senator Stratton. But my house and my business aren't places where someone of your, let's say, philosophies, typically shows up on a rainy evening."

"I would think it's always a rainy evening when someone of my so-called 'philosophies' appears at your door. More dramatically fitting that way. May I come in?"

"Actually, I'm not sure. I don't need a witch hunter in my home. Is that why you're here, to call your righteous troops in to attack me?" She glanced down. I'd hit a nerve.

Her mouth pursed as she formulated her reply. "I would think your line of work, as mine, has left you with few illusions about the public faces of celebrities. Regardless of what my supporters may think, I need your services, and I've heard you're the epitome of discretion. Are you alone?"

"My friend is here, but I'm not sure I want to be involved with any of your motivations. I have a few scruples and aiding the *mishegoss* of the right isn't on my to-do list."

She took a breath and placed a hand on the wall of the porch. "We are far from crazy. I know some Yiddish too. I assure you that any involvement with me will not help my supporters' campaign to recapture the glory of our country."

"I'm not sure I believe that, but come in. This is against my better judgment, though. I'll send my friend away for a while. You've got one hour with me, and it will be expensive."

"If you can help me, it will be worth more than you can charge."

"That's what I'm worried about."

I led her to the living room, wanting to avoid the mess in the library. While she made herself comfortable on the couch, I found Fitch and directed her to a roadhouse several miles away to pick up some broasted chicken with jo jo potatoes.

"Is that edible?"

"Trust me, you'll love it and the roadhouse. It's a cultural experience. Be back in one hour and fifteen minutes. I might have more work for you. Oh, and would you stop at the mini-mart and grab a pack of those vitamin C suckies? I think my immune system needs work. And, Fitch, no picking up women."

Looking hostile, she stomped out to the garage where she'd parked her vehicle. I heard her mutter something about never hitting on a woman while wearing denim. Everybody has their standards, even Fitch.

When I returned to the living room, Elizabeth Stratton, minus her iconic makeup and chignon, sat on my couch like royalty. I wanted to slap her hypocritical face, but I was inexplicably compelled to carry out this session. It wasn't the money. Something else drove me forward, probably just dumb nosiness, my perennial Achilles' heel.

"You're wondering why someone like me would choose to meet with someone like you, Ms. Rosten. Rest assured. I believe your work is nothing less than Satanism, but it brings results, so my sources tell me. I'll get in bed with the devil to achieve my goals and, I believe, so have you. Pragmatism accomplishes great things, in my experience."

"Wrong, Ms. Stratton. There's nothing Satan-like about my work." At least I privately hoped there wasn't. I didn't know where my abilities came from or even if they were diabolically supplied. But I had the intuition that they were just my legacy, like my wavy black hair and five feet eight inch stature.

As I shuffled the worn cards, I set my usual ground rules. "Please stay relaxed and don't ask me to perform stunts like naming what's in your purse or your secretary's mother's maiden name. I don't do parlor tricks. If I remain quiet for several seconds to several minutes, you'll need to keep still, or you'll distract me from what I'm learning. Whatever information I give you is yours to do with as you will, meaning I have no investment in the outcome of your life. However, if you need my 'reorganization' services, we will discuss what outcome you wish to achieve, and I'll do my best to make that happen. Just don't object to my methods. Your ignorance safeguards both of us. Do you have any questions before we begin?"

Typically, at this point in a reading, new clients would become nervous and second thoughts would cavort in their heads. But not Elizabeth Stratton. She remained icy, distant, and annoying. I had to admit, though, she was dangerously attractive. She studied me with an indefinable look that reminded me she had been a renowned attorney before her political life began several years earlier.

"And what happens if your efforts fail? Or you get caught? Need I worry?"

"That's never happened, and I've worked for clients who, believe it or not, are under the media microscope more closely than you. But to set your mind at ease, remember if I do get discovered and reveal who I'm working for, my career ends right along with yours. And I really don't want that to happen. I enjoy my privileged medical benefits too much."

"And your fee?"

"Will be refunded in full if you aren't satisfied. If someone in your position is exposed as my client, you'll definitely need every penny you can get just to handle the hate mail from your disappointed groupies." I couldn't resist the jab. Her constituents were everything that was wrong about our country. I didn't want her to even consider that I was enamored of her, like the poor souls who thought she was the second coming of the messiah.

She was a poised woman because she didn't flinch. "Will your distaste for me interfere with your effectiveness? Believe me, any verbal punch you throw is nothing I haven't weathered hundreds of times before. I'm here for your services. Can you put your misguided politics aside and deliver results?"

For the first time in my career, I had to consider her question. I'd worked with some extremely unsavory clients without feeling any indignation regarding what they did for a living or behind closed doors. But with this woman, someone I intuitively knew was on the wrong side of things, someone who manipulated ignorant, underinformed people with her looks and ability to quip trite motivational sound bites, could I stay aloof from all that? I was disturbed to feel shaking anger and considered calling off the reading and sending her back to her lair. But something, some compulsion, kept me going along with her, even though my emotions were far from serene. In fact, every Jewish pogrom warning bell clanged within me; my heritage reminded me where danger resided.

Elizabeth Stratton had come to me as a client. I had never refused a client, not their assignments and not their money. I wasn't ready to change what had been a successful formula.

Had I ended the session right then, everything would have been different. All the events that happened after could have been avoided. I should have remembered the wisdom of my people: She who makes a promise runs in debt.

Chapter Five

Something about having the infamous Senator Stratton, conservative presidential candidate, as a client destroyed my usual objectivity. My massive intuitive senses were clanging. I'd always felt the woman was a fraud, but sitting in her presence dredged up emotions I'd never experienced with a client: anger, hostility, disgust, and even fear. But there was something irresistible about the woman, a boatload of charismatic intelligence matched with the allure of power. I was beginning to understand why some voters were swayed by her malicious rhetoric. That made me indignant for the people who really couldn't see through the manipulation.

When I glanced at the card spread on the table, I saw little that was remarkable except the Knight of Swords card. The picture depicted an armored knight waving his vicious double-edged sword and glaring at me with concentrated hate. A card of intellectual aggression, using one's mind to attack a problem.

Then it happened: the vision. But this time it was different, more complicated.

I found myself standing at the back of a press conference, all attention focused on an empty podium. The occupants of the crowded room were waiting for someone to make an announcement. I pressed my back into the corner and waited only for a few minutes when the silent crowd parted to let someone through. I saw the back of a blond head move through the reporters to reach the podium. Although her head was lowered, she walked with purpose and strength, and didn't falter when she climbed the few steps to the small stage that held the podium. It was Laura Bishop.

The reporters were now murmuring. Some spoke into their phones or voice recorders.

Laura was dressed in a rumpled sweat suit. It seemed her arm was injured and there were wounds on her face. Underneath her other arm she held a large book that looked like it held loose-leaf pages. She stood at the podium, her eyes bruised from fatigue, and barely registered the crowd. The reporters began to hurl questions at her. The sound in the vision didn't allow me to hear the complete questions.

"Ms. Bishop, do you have proof—"

"Miss Bishop, do you expect the American people to believe—"

"Do you really think a candidate of such stature—"

"Our sources reveal that you were—"

I knew she was having difficulty maintaining her composure as she continually swept her hair behind one ear and kept her eyes on her rumpled notes. When she finally looked up, her eyes searched the room and locked on mine.

And with every fiber of my being, I wanted her.

My entire body was smashed into the room's corner as if I had no skeleton, only soggy flesh.

The High Priestess's voice rang in my head. "Meddler. Your mission begins now."

I opened my eyes to see the storybook painted sky of the Theater. Everything hurt, my torso, appendages, and head. Even through the pain, the physical desire for Laura Bishop hadn't subsided. I had to resist pressing my hands to my throbbing crotch.

To my left was Pento, motionless like a mannequin, but as soon as I made a scraping sound with my foot, he came alive and looked at me.

"Some freako theme park this is," I said.

"Ah, back again, I see. Good then. I have something to show you." He wasn't smiling as before, but I grabbed his dry, gloved hand when he offered to pull me out of the sand.

"Where are we now?" I brushed the sand from my pants. Sand? Well, at least pseudo sand. I felt the whatever-it-was slide into the lamb's wool slippers that I'd been wearing for coziness during the reading. "I hope you realize I'm not dressed for action, Pento."

"Your attire is of no consequence to me. You have covering on your feet, a particularly human affectation. Throughout the cosmos, you are the only ones who deem footwear important. The others laugh at you, you know."

"What others? Why are shoes funny?"

"You are not the only ones trying to get by in your paltry world. There are countless others in countless worlds. You are just the only ones who wear shoes. It is humorous."

"I'm not laughing, and don't expect me to do any schlepping without my arch supports."

"Schlepping? Arch supports?"

"Never mind. What is it you want to show me? I have a kind of important reading going on right now." I sat back down and emptied the uniform-sized grains of sand from my slippers.

"Yes, your, what do you call it…'client'? That is why we have summoned you. This is emergency training. The Malignity has made moves we failed to predict."

"Wait. My client is the Malignity? Elizabeth Stratton? Why am I not surprised? Is she my adversary?"

"For such a handsome human specimen, you ask many questions. You make many assumptions with your questions, so I have difficulty deciding which one to answer first. Therefore, let me illustrate what your challenge is, and you can decide how to meet it."

"But I thought you would decide and I'd just carry out your wishes." I stood back up and brushed the manufactured sand off my butt.

"We decide for you? No. We never decide for humans. We may inform them, guide them a little, even place an opportunity within their reach. But we never decide for them. That is not how it is designed for humans."

"How what is designed?"

"Free choice, of course."

"You mean all this is a choice?" I waved my hand toward the sand dune that obscured my ability to get my bearings.

"Oh no, we make the Theaters. Then we bring adept humans, those belonging to the correct lines, to Theaters that best suit the humans' talents. Humans make their choices about how to operate within their particular Theaters. It is the cosmic law, one we agreed upon eons ago. We try to settle differences with the Malignity within a Theater, using the lines. If things are not settled there, then it gets uncomfortable for humans in their world. We try to watch out for you, but your choices often do keep us from helping."

"So are you going to supply a menu of choices? Or do I make them up as I go? What's a 'line'?"

"Oh, you already have the menu. You hardly need my help with a menu."

"This is too much, Pento. I'm confused. I want to think

about all this later. Show me what you need to show me, and I'll get back to my client."

He pointed to the top of the dune, and I started to climb it, sliding back a foot for every two feet I gained. I could hear waves crashing somewhere in the direction I was heading.

"I would not go bumbling into plain sight if I were you, pretty damsel," Pento called after me.

"You can call me Dev," I said over my shoulder.

When I neared the summit of the dune, I stayed low and peeked over. Spread in front of me, like a vast museum painting, was an ocean beach, endless and loud. But it lacked dimension, like the backdrop of a play. It was lit by unearthly light, not quite sunlight, more like the lamps used to illuminate a movie set, fake but bright. The water stretched to the horizon with sizable waves that looked more artificial the farther away they stretched. In the far distance, the sea was like the work of a delusional impressionist painter. I wondered where Pento was getting his information about what the earth looked like.

Far to my left, a quarter mile down the beach, there was activity. Human forms doing something I couldn't make out. I decided to stay behind the dunes and move closer to the people on the beach but avoid their spotting me. First, I removed my slippers, deciding that bare feet would operate better in the unstable faux sand than loose lamb's wool slippers. I placed the slippers on top of the dune, hoping that they would be easier to find when I returned. I looked behind to see if Pento would follow me. Pento was gone.

Courage was not an aspiration as far as I was concerned. I didn't want to go it alone in a place created for some vague need that had barely been explained to me. But curiosity was one of my favorite motivators, so I decided to see what had been created there on the beach for my personal enlightenment. At least, I hoped it would be enlightening.

I scrambled along the land side of the dunes, keeping my head below their crests so that I couldn't be seen. When I determined I had gone far enough to be fairly close to the action on the beach, I slowly made my way up the back of a dune, trying to avoid making noise. Then I remembered that the hollow ocean roar would drown out any sound I made.

It took me several moments to adjust my eyes and believe what I was witnessing. Blades jammed into the sand, eight medieval swords, the kind I can barely lift, encircled a woman bound in ropes. She was blindfolded, dressed in a loose white gown, and tied to a large stake. She struggled against her bondage. Her lips were saying something, but I was too far away to hear. Behind the spiked swords, beneath the blindfold was Laura Bishop. Then my attention was centered on the armored knight lurking outside the ring of standing swords.

As I watched him, he hefted his own lethal sword and swung it around his head, never taking his eyes from Laura Bishop. Even from where I hid, I heard the swoosh, swoosh of his weapon as he wielded it around and around, readying for a strike. He planned to execute her.

Laura cried out, and my attention returned to her. She was wearing the same clothes she wore at the press conference, battered sweatpants and a soiled T-shirt. She was participating in some bizarre tableau of the Eight of Swords, a minor tarot card, but one with threatened violence. The violence could sometimes emerge from one's inability to change an ethic or philosophy. There was nothing philosophic about the scene before me. It was lethal.

Like a heroic fool, I pushed myself over the top of the dune and bellowed at the knight. "Hey, stop! Look over here." I skidded on my rear all the way down the dune. When I jarred to a stop, I clambered up and ran toward the knight. He was within a few inches of taking off Laura's head. Her hair riffled from the air displaced by the swiping giant sword.

Without missing a step or a swing, the knight turned toward me, away from Laura. Like an automaton, he walked toward me, face hidden by his helmet's facemask. I could see his eyes, though. They were lifeless and remorseless, committed to my destruction without an afterthought.

"Yeah, come get me, you piece of dreck!" I turned and sprinted down the beach feeling my toes desperately pushing into squeaky fake sand. I glanced behind. He was following me, leaving Laura safe for the moment.

I ran faster, then glanced back again. He was advancing at the same unyielding speed. I had time, and I didn't want him to refocus on Laura. My need to save her overwhelmed any desire to save myself. That's new, was my fleeting thought.

The cramp hit in the arch of my left foot. Pain steamed through my foot and ankle. I cried out, stopped, looked down at my foot, then looked up into the face of Elizabeth Stratton.

My slippers were on still smarting feet. My woven Afghani rug was under the coffee table between Elizabeth and me. No ocean, no sword-wielding knight, and no Laura Bishop. Had all that been real?

"Who's the blonde, Senator?" I wasn't about to give her Laura Bishop's name.

She watched me, eyes narrowed, for several seconds. "So you really do have some uncanny ability. My advisor wasn't trying to set me up. Describe this blonde you mentioned."

"I don't think I have to. But she has something on you. You're worried she'll go public with whatever it is. And you want me to stop her."

"She's not much of a threat to my campaign. I just want to know if she needs a small derailment. Since you are under the impression she has something on me, then it's clear she needs to be…distracted. I think that's where you come in, Ms. Rosten. Isn't that what you do? Distract people?"

"With the proper inducement, I can sometimes send people down another path. I make no guarantees, but I usually achieve my clients' aims."

"And you do so without causing harm?" Her look of uncertainty told me more than anything she said.

"Depends upon your definition of harm. But I never physically threaten a subject, just realign a trajectory."

"By what methods, may I ask?"

"That's privileged information, Senator. What is the woman's name?"

"Bishop, Laura Bishop. She's an attorney in Seattle. I have a file here with her particulars." She reached into her purse and drew out a little flash drive and set it on the table. "Oh, and here is my first payment to you. I'll give you a second equal payment on completion of your assignment. That assignment is to persuade Laura Bishop to remain silent with regard to any information she has about me. And I don't want her harmed. If it's traced back to me, well, you know the ramifications as well as I."

I didn't think it necessary to respond. Besides, I was dumbfounded because she placed a cashier's check for $125,000 on the table.

"When you've completed your job to my satisfaction, Ms. Rosten, I will give you another check for the same amount. However, if you fail, or our meeting here tonight becomes public, you will not only lose the next payment, you will lose your entire business." She looked around the living room. "And it appears your business is extremely lucrative. Do we have a deal?"

"Let me look into it. See if it's a job within my skill set. If not, I will destroy the check. As for your visit here tonight, all my clients are on a confidential list kept only in my head. To expose you would possibly expose other clients, so, no, I won't be calling the press for a tell-all. No matter what. Is that sufficient?"

I didn't pick up the check or the flash drive. I really couldn't take my eyes off this woman. She was the standard bearer for people so deluded, they would follow her into a snake pit, believing her to be a woman of God. She was a fraud, and I wasn't one to question my intuition anymore. She was repugnant to me, but I wasn't going to fully show her my distaste any more than I already had. It was a lot of money she was waving around. Maybe I could fashion a way to achieve Stratton's goals, acquire a quarter million dollars, and see Laura Bishop, in person, for the first time in years. It was an irresistible moment of personal and professional dishonor.

"I know you don't want to work with me, Ms. Rosten. But let me assure you that I have always been an unwavering supporter for the Jews. They will always find an ally with me. It will be worth it for you to help me…for your people."

I could tell she was sincere about supporting Israel, but then the cynical caveat "for the moment" passed through my head. She meant what she said, and she always said exactly what she felt, or so her campaign claimed. What Elizabeth Stratton didn't see was her shadow self, her blind spot. Elizabeth Stratton compartmentalized her feelings and, therefore, her rhetoric. That was how she could seduce people into believing every incendiary word she said. She believed it herself, until the moment arrived when a particular political stance was no longer convenient. Then, like discarding underwear, she donned a new, more crowd-rallying stance and railed on. If it ever served her purpose, she'd put Jews in the crosshairs too. I knew that better than she did.

I let her out my front door and watched her pull her hood over her hair, as protection from both the rain and recognition. Her black SUV waited in the driveway. I could tell by the barely discernable little puff of exhaust trickling out of the tailpipe that it was running. Someone had been waiting for her.

I went back into the living room and stood over the check and flash drive warring with myself. Finally, I took the check, folded it, and tucked it into a small, never-used drawer in the coffee table. I put the flash drive in my pocket.

I flopped down on the couch and thought about Laura Bishop, vexed by how my heart rate increased when I envisioned her face, her eyes as she looked at me with trust, more than trust, during the press conference. I became even more disturbed when I realized that I needed to find her, not for Elizabeth Stratton, not for money, but for me.

❖

After several minutes of torturing myself over Laura Bishop, I heard a door slam and movement in the kitchen. I jumped in alarm and then remembered Fitch was around, and I'd sent her on a food errand. Food felt like a great idea.

"Goddamn, son of a bitch, Rosten. What kind of people live around here? What is this, Heil Hitler Land?" Fitch slammed a couple sacks on the counter and squeezed their tops into balls.

"What? What happened?'

"A couple of skinheads, low-IQ goons followed me to the roadhouse. They were driving some fancy black Mercedes SUV. I could tell it was a Mercedes because they practically rode my bumper all the way there, and I could see them in the rearview. The bastards."

"A black Mercedes?" I was certain the SUV waiting for Elizabeth Stratton was a Mercedes. She wasn't a Kia kind of woman. "When did they start following you?"

"A little ways down the road, after I left here. And they tailgated me all the way to the roadhouse. I parked the car and watched them park several cars away. I'm not usually scared, not my M.O., but these guys had cruelty pasted all over them, a trait easy for me to spot. They watched me go into the tavern, and I couldn't resist flipping them off before I went inside. I heard one of them scream 'cunt' as the roadhouse door slammed."

"Oh, Fitch, I'm sorry. I suspect they had something to do with my client, if the cars match."

Fitch paced the kitchen and waved her arms. "Hey, that's not all that happened, not by a long shot."

"I'm not sure I'm ready to hear this."

"Listen, if these guys have anything to do with your client, you're in deep shit. In fact, I'm probably in deep shit too, just for being here."

"Tell me exactly what happened." My hands began to shake with a wild blend of fear and anger.

"When I was in the roadhouse, I ordered a beer and the take-out food. I downed the beer fast, just to calm my nerves. I went into the bathroom to make sure my piece was loaded and ready for action." Fitch patted the belly bag she always wore when she went out. I had assumed it contained keys, a wallet, and maybe a spare set of nipple clamps.

"Piece?"

"My gun…my pistol?"

"You carry a gun, Fitch? There's a gun in my house? Loaded?" I staggered back and plopped on a stool.

"Hey, I'm always armed. I know too much about too many important people. As a matter of fact, so do you. You should be armed, Dev. You're a walking target."

"I'm a Jewish American girl. What do I know from guns?" I stared at the floor trying to cope with the truth Fitch was handing me. "Tell me the rest."

"When I went out to the parking lot, carrying our dinner, several people were standing around my car. My beautiful Jag's alarm was blaring. As I got closer, I could see the passenger window was smashed. Some man said, 'That your car? Sorry, lady.' I hate being called 'lady.' It's so condescending."

"Never mind that. Why was your car alarm blaring?"

"I looked into the smashed window. Those skinhead assholes had stuck a meat cleaver into the seat and left it there."

"A meat cleaver. Why a meat cleaver?"

"To scare me. I use them all the time for the same purpose, only I never really cleave anything. Anything that's alive, anyway." Fitch stopped pacing and leaned against the counter, hand over her belly bag.

"You use meat cleavers to scare people?"

"Well, yeah, I have this one favorite scene where I'm the butcher and—"

"That's fine. I get the idea." I'd been shocked enough for one night and didn't need Fitch's graphic description of her BDSM activities. Feeling like a wimpy vanilla wafer, I smelled the broasted chicken and remembered I wanted to eat. "Let's have some food, and we'll figure out how to get your car fixed. Did you get the vitamin C suckies?"

Fitch gave me an I'm-going-to-murder-you look. Not only was she armed, she knew her way around a meat cleaver. I let the suckies go.

Chapter Six

My policy was to avoid face-to-face contact with any of the "targets" my clients paid me to divert. But I needed to see Laura Bishop again. My questions about Stratton couldn't be answered without her. Why was each cell of my body a microscopic magnet tugging toward its anchor in Laura? I wasn't given to getting the vapors over a pretty woman, so I knew this draw to her had to be investigated. I'd done a reading for her eight years earlier and recently glimpsed her a few times in my visions. Why her? And the genesis of my visions was still unknown to me.

Elizabeth Stratton's bizarre but lucrative visit created more questions. What was her connection to Laura Bishop? How far could I go with my methods for persuading Laura to not expose whatever it was Stratton was hiding? What did Stratton want to hide? I felt the link between Stratton and Bishop was obvious, hiding in front of me like a refrigerator magnet that becomes part of the kitchen scenery and, therefore, unseen.

I knew somehow it was all related to the macabre High Priestess with no fingernails, but I couldn't contact her or Pento at will, at least not yet. The video Fitch had made of me while I was visiting the Theater would have to wait. I had other work to do.

❖

The morning after the Stratton visit was a Monday. Fitch and I studied the information about Laura Bishop that Elizabeth Stratton had left with me on the flash drive. The facts were remarkably thin with little except education and professional background on the successful attorney. However, there was one piece of pay dirt, the fridge magnet. I was a little angry at myself for not remembering the key piece of information I'd forgotten about Laura Bishop.

"Damn, if I'd remembered that Laura Bishop and Elizabeth Stratton were working in the same firm ten years ago, I could have asked Stratton better questions." We were bending over my little laptop reading the files together.

"Meyers, Gaines, and Stratton, that's some high-powered legal firm. It's now called Meyers and Gaines. They must've dropped the Stratton part when she entered politics. Dev, call Stratton and dig a little deeper into the work connection between her and Bishop."

"Uh, I can't." I closed the file and got up to refill my coffee. "Stratton didn't leave any contact information, and I was too *fartootst* to remember to ask. I normally don't let confusion cause me to make mistakes."

"Well, not many people have a harridan of hell show up on the doorstep of their secluded island house. Had I known who it was, I'd never have gone to get that food. I would've hid out and spied on her. It's the least she deserves for causing so much hatred in this country." Fitch's eyes had grown dark, and I worried for her slaves when she got back home. Then I remembered they liked it when she got rough.

"Oy." Fitch looked at me and I felt obliged to redirect

my thoughts. "So what do you think Laura Bishop has on Elizabeth Stratton?"

"Well, I intend to find out. Maybe Stratton had some shady dealings at the law firm, and Bishop discovered them. Bishop's holding Stratton hostage with the information. Stranger things have happened," Fitch said.

"That's probably what it is. My question is what should I do about it? Do I just waylay Laura Bishop, or should we find out what the information is that Bishop is holding?"

"Rosten, your job is to deter Bishop, but my job is always getting the information. How about you do your part, and I'll back you up with what I can find out. If Meyers, Gaines, and formerly Stratton has the usual lame information protection like other law firms, I'll be into its files in no time. I'll start when I get back home to my equipment."

Fitch ate five pieces of butter-drenched toast while I drank my protein smoothie with a vitamin C boost. Then we reviewed the visions I had the previous evening. She was remarkably relaxed with the idea that I was getting information from "elsewhere." I chalked it up to the fact that Fitch's world was so out of the norm that she had a high tolerance for strange.

"The first time you saw Bishop was when you did a reading for her about eight years ago. The next time was when you were with that Pento dude. And again last night. She was standing in front of a press conference in your…what do you call it…other-worldly travel? Tell me what she was saying again."

"I don't think she spoke while I was there. What I saw were reporters, some hostile and some just salivating for a great story, who were questioning the veracity of whatever she had announced. She looked pretty beaten up, but she looked directly into my eyes. Then everything switched, and I saw her on that beach in the Theater. She was tied and blindfolded with some crazed robotic knight-type swinging a sword at her."

"My kind of action. And this took place when?"

"That's just it, Fitch. These are always visions of future possibilities, if things aren't redirected. So no press conference has taken place, and Stratton wants me to make sure it doesn't. I'm beginning to think the things I experience in the Theater are something other than real. I'm missing an obvious piece of information about them."

"Something other than real? Like a metaphor or clue? She's in danger, but then again, maybe not. I'm betting this Laura Bishop has something apocalyptical on Elizabeth Stratton. How delicious. I know a lot of dirt on a lot of important people, but most of it isn't any worse than what I do in my own dungeon. Any scandal on Stratton, well, that would be worth some serious influence. It could be dangerous, given the stupefied loyalty of her followers."

"Yeah, it's worth influence and money. You should see the wad she left me. Of course, you'll get your share if you want to work with me on this." I always paid Fitch, even if she was one of the richest women in the universe.

"Don't need the money, honey. I want the information. So where do you think I should start? Want me to investigate Laura Bishop while she was at Meyers, Gaines, and Stratton? Do a serious deep excavation on Elizabeth Stratton? You tell me and I'll do it."

"Stratton, for sure but not immediately. Let's focus on Laura Bishop first. You do the whole workup like you usually do for me: family and its skeletons, Bishop and her secrets, whatever you can find. I want to wade straight into the lion's den. I'm going to visit Laura Bishop." I was hoping Fitch wouldn't notice how excited I became at the thought of meeting Laura.

Later, Fitch and I swept the shattered chunks of glass from inside her car. Then we taped some heavy plastic over the window gap. When she was ready to leave for her dungeon and one-woman spy operation, I promised her I'd pay for her car damage. She just smiled as she engaged her ignition.

"Worry not. I'll take it to my dealer. The secretary there is one of mine. She'll make sure the window is replaced, the seat repaired, and my boots are licked. It'll be an errand of pleasure."

"Oy, you leave me with no comebacks," I said. She backed out the car and left me to my own muddle.

With Fitch gone, I packed my belongings and closed down Tranquility until I could return. I made arrangements with my usual housekeeper and a local security company to take care of the house. My instincts told me that when my business arrangement with Elizabeth Stratton was completed, I'd need Tranquility more than I ever had before.

As I rode the forty-minute ferry back to the mainland, I nestled my exhausted body into one of the comfortable chairs inside the indoor observation deck of the ferry. Determined gulls flew next to the rain-spattered window, trying to attract the attention of any passenger willing to step outside, risk drenching, and share a potato chip. Ocean smells wafted through the doors accessing the promenade deck. The rocking hum of the ferry relaxed me, and I realized my body muscles had been wound tight for days.

I shifted position in the chair so I could lay my head on the back rest, something I rarely did because the thought of some lice-covered nature hippie having used the chair previous to my claiming it usually gacked me.

Though my body was exhausted, my mind continued its incessant churn. Eyes closed, I pondered my ethical dilemma, an unusual and uncomfortable task for me.

I had taken Stratton's money and assured her that I could derail whatever path Laura Bishop was on. Normally, that would take a few strategic phone calls, or text messages, or vague threats couched in phony solicitors' letters. Sometimes I would use Fitch's hacker skills and cause just enough cyber havoc to waylay a target. That usually entailed some fiddling with social media or posting damaging altered photos or videos. Nothing seriously harmful, unless my targets ignored the message. They never did.

In the case of Laura Bishop, could this be the mission the High Priestess had conscripted me to execute? What was Pento's role in my current circumstances? Was Elizabeth Stratton connected to Malignity or was Laura Bishop?

"Maybe," I murmured to myself, "but probably not."

Then I remembered Laura's eyes when she looked at me over the heads of the reporters. She was afraid, desperate even. She had looked to me for help, yet we had only met once. A chaos of emotions: desire, compassion, even anger welled within me. I heard the scratchy laugh of the High Priestess, and my rage ignited when I felt the familiar impossible squeeze upon my skull. When the constriction eased, I opened my eyes and found myself on the cold marble floor before the High Priestess's dais.

I pushed myself to a sitting position and gave her the most disgusted look I could muster while groveling on the floor. I supposed it was fruitless and made no impression on her. It was then I realized what she reminded me of. Her face was like one of those silly movies where someone spies on people by peering through eyeholes cut into a walled painting. The face doesn't move, but the eyes follow the quarry. Something was *in* her. The facade I was allowed to see was a shell, a grim costume. Something else inhabited the form.

"And this is the most you'll ever see, human half-wit. It is all you could tolerate."

"Then tell me," I said as I hobbled to my feet, "is this place real? Am I really here, or is this a vision?"

"Let's just say it's real enough for our purposes." She scratched out another chuckle. "We can't tell you how to respond, but we can send you in the proper directions. Offer signposts and maybe, miraculously, you'll make the proper choices."

"First of all, if you keep treating me like a schmuck, I'll respond like a schmuck. Secondly, why not just tell me what you want me to do and be done with it? I carry out whatever chore you want this dumb human to complete, and we can both be on our cheery way. I really hate that transition torture you make me go through every time I have to see you or Pento."

"Pento?" Her unwrinkled, nail-less fingers were twitching slightly, like a puppet someone was trying to learn to operate.

I looked away from her perverted hand. "Yeah, the guy who smirks, makes useless comments, and shows me bizarre tableaus."

She stared at me for a long moment then her eyes, somehow, darkened or intensified. "Now, I have something to say to you, so clear the moldering cobwebs from between your ears and listen."

"My three cells of gray matter are at attention."

"I suppose that was human sarcasm. Typical. But since we need you, I won't punish you for insolence. Hear this: the Malignity has advanced swiftly during this time. As usual, it wields the double-edged sword of dogma and fear. The areas of your world we thought the Malignity couldn't assail are now under siege, and you bumbling humans have no idea. However, we have many warrior lines and a few meddler lines like you. The warriors are overt, but the meddlers, by necessity and nature, work alone and behind the world stage."

"Look, your, uh, Highness, I'm not really cut out for saving myself, much less the world. I have no idea what you mean by 'lines.' And something called the Malignity? That sounds like a disease, and if there is anything that scares me off, it's disease. One time in college, I got a roaring case of mononucleosis and since then—"

"Enough!" She did a convincing, if jerky, eye roll. "You have no choice in this matter. Everything is in motion. Remember, human, what the cards have taught you. Go away. Use your skills for what they were designed." I saw her hand flick. I was hurled again against the pillar behind her, and everything went dark for a couple seconds.

Then I was standing, facing a stone wall. Actually, my nose was only an inch from it, and I stumbled backward. I tripped over a large loose stone and fell with a vicious bang on my tailbone. I lay groaning and stared at the fake blue sky of the Theater. Convinced I had cracked a vertebra or two, I yearned for an icepack.

The synthetic blue sky was partly obliterated by the wall that rose above me the distance of maybe ten or eleven stories. It was old, or at least it was manufactured to look old. There were green and orange fuzzy lichen patches dotting the wall. The structure replicated an ancient keep where castle residents would gather for protection and fight off invaders.

"It is one of my best creations, damsel. What do you think? Does it pass for the real thing?" Pento was standing over me with a proud grin.

"So help me up, already, and I'll give your work a critical review." I held my hand up, and he grasped it with his gloved hand. When I stood, I inspected his glove for a moment and asked, "Hey, Pento, do you have fingernails?"

"Do I have fingernails? I did not need any to build this tower. It is completely stone…or like stone."

"No, not construction nails, fingernails, like these." I held up my hand to show him my usually bitten nails and lurched. "Shit! Shit! Shit!"

"What is troubling you?"

"Where are my fingernails? Goddamn it, Pento, I need my nails. I can't touch anything without fingernails. It gives me the willies."

"I cannot create what I have not seen. I am not sure what you mean by 'willies.'"

"Is everyone in this…this Theater like us? No fingernails, no breath, no whatever is supposed to make us alive? Make us human?" I was holding my hands straight down at my sides, avoiding the possibility of seeing my nauseating fingertips again.

"Oh, that other one, he whom you saw on the beach. He creates his share of things, like the swords, but I do not look closely at them. Maybe they have these…fingernails."

"So do you create the High Priestess too? Is she a product of your imagination and carpentry skills?"

"The High Priestess? You must mean our Lady? Oh, no, no, no. She gives me leave to create the Theater. I am hers, her ally, her knight." He did a twitchy imitation of a proud soldier.

"And who is the other knight allied with, the one with the big nasty sword?"

Pento shook his head, confused. "Who is he allied with? You should know. You must know He-Who-Comes-Before. If you don't know him, all my work is for naught."

"He-Who?" A metallic clanking shattered our conversation. An enormous sword shot from the tower and clattered within a yard from where we stood. I looked up just in time to see an ironclad knight pitch backward over the edge of the tower and crumple on top of the sword. He didn't move. It was the same knight I'd encountered on the beach, the one who was going to execute Laura Bishop.

"Get me out! Get some help!" The shouting came from above. I looked up again. There she was, blond hair tangled, eyes wild, yelling something. I focused finally and heard her shout. I turned to Pento. He was gone.

"How do I get up there?" I hollered back as I started running around the tower, looking for an entrance. Finally, my chance to meet Laura Bishop.

There was no door, no stairway. The fallen knight had vanished along with Pento. I was alone, just over a hundred feet from Laura Bishop, and couldn't find my way to her. I stopped running and looked up to her. She reached to me and tears streaked her cheeks.

"Please, help me, please." Even from that distance, it was obvious that her eyes were wretched with fear. It was unclear if she was really looking at me or at something else in my vicinity.

Something tripped me to the ground, and I was flat on my back again. Everything shook like in a low-budget movie simulating an earthquake by shaking the camera. The artificial ground beneath me trembled. The tower began rocking back and forth like a kid's block tower. It was collapsing and I was right under it. Laura's blanched face swayed with the tower as I tried to crawl away, helpless to save her. With a defeated moan, the tower toppled, carrying Laura Bishop with it. Her scream and the rumble of the tower made me cover my doomed head with my arm while I waited for stones from the tower to flatten me.

And I waited. I lifted my arm from my eyes and found myself sitting in the San Juan ferry as it docked at Anacortes. A blast of the ferry horn mimicked the groaning mangling of the tower. The other passengers were returning to their vehicles, engaged in delighted conversation. I was almost alone on the passenger deck. One aggrieved gull ranted at me through the window.

I glanced at the exit to the car deck and saw a heavily armed security guard staring intently at me.

CHAPTER SEVEN

The prime attraction of my getaway house, Tranquility, was its isolation from the rest of the distracting world. But that was also its curse. Usually, when I was there, I'd use my laptop or my mobile device to catch up on culture and the news. But my immersion into the cards, Fitch's visit, and the meeting with Elizabeth Stratton distracted me from the outside world.

When I left the house that Sunday, I had no idea that the entire Washington State Ferry System was under siege. Dogs and federal agents were combing through each car that rode a ferry, and the agents were asking passengers questions, mostly about who they had seen while on board. By the time they got to me, I had an anxious belly and could feel a stiff headache coming on.

After studying my driver's license, they rummaged in the trunk of my Lexus and stared into my backseat. The agent was all business with her heavily equipped belt that included a gun. She was not a woman to cozy up to, so I mirrored her seriousness.

"Ms. Rosten, I'm going to show you an artist's drawing of a man. Could you tell me if you saw him anywhere on this boat today?" She produced a clipboard and held it before me.

"Take a good look and think hard. Did you see him today anywhere?"

My hand pressed on the open door of my car where I had rested it. I needed to sit down. I needed to breathe. The picture was of a burly bald man with a nondescript face, but his muscular neck sported a swastika. It was the man from the vision I'd had eight years previously. The man who wanted to kill Laura Bishop.

"Uh, uh…" I had no words. How could I tell her that I'd seen him in my vision years ago?

The agent was watching me closely. "Do you know this man, Ms. Rosten? It's important you tell me what you know."

I had to shake off my shock. "Oh, I'm sorry, Officer. It's the swastika. I'm Jewish, you see. Holocaust history in my family, you know. So seeing a swastika is sometimes upsetting. And I'm a little under the weather anyway."

She watched me for a few painful seconds, then nodded. "Okay, well if you can think of anything to tell us, here's my card. Call me."

"Sure, of course, Officer." She turned to walk away, but I reached and tapped her arm. She swirled around and I asked, "What did this man do? Can you tell me?"

"He murdered three people at the Smith Tower last night and was last seen on a Washington State ferry." She turned and strode to the next car.

Show no emotion, I thought. Don't let her see you scared. I fell back into my car seat and thought about the trip to the Theater I'd just experienced. A crumbling tower, just like the tarot card called the Tower. It was often interpreted as the destruction of the world or lifestyle we've become familiar with.

"Oh shit," I murmured, "three people dead." The murders

were in the Smith Tower. The Smith Tower housed Laura Bishop's office.

I turned on my phone and tried to call Fitch. No answer, so I left a terse message for her to call me about the Smith Tower incident.

I activated the Internet browser on my phone to see what the press was saying about the murders. Very little. Three people brutally murdered the previous evening at the Smith Tower. No names released pending notification of the next of kin. The investigation was open and ongoing. In short, they knew nothing. There wasn't even a mention of the man having been seen on a ferry or the identity of the witness who helped authorities devise a drawing of the suspect.

I needed Fitch to dig around, and Fitch was incommunicado, probably swaggering around her dungeon delivering punishment to a devoted and willing slave.

My anxiety escalated, and heartburn sizzled inside my esophagus. I would have begged one of the security officers for some Maalox, but they looked just as pained as I did. I pressed the acupressure point on my stomach that sometimes worked to relieve my chronic heartburn.

I burrowed into my car seat and settled in for the wait to exit the ferry. To escape the torture of my own mind and fears for Laura, I thought about what I had learned while at Tranquility and what I hadn't learned. Surely, Laura Bishop and Elizabeth Stratton were connected in a way that made Stratton vulnerable, probably politically. Bishop was an attorney, so maybe she had represented Stratton at one time and learned sensitive information. Maybe they were related by family? Hopefully, Fitch would uncover some of that information.

The thought of Fitch reminded me of the vandalism done to her car. Nothing had been stolen, so it was either random mischief by some losers or a warning. I wasn't hopeful of the former motive. Fitch's description of the stalkers' car appeared to match the description of the black SUV that was waiting for Stratton when she left my house. The car vandalism was probably a warning. But why? Why would Stratton feel like she needed to warn Fitch or, more likely, me? I was a paragon of discretion.

Laura Bishop. I rested my forehead on the steering wheel and groaned, "Oy, yoy, yoy." The thought of her sent my heart into schoolgirl palpitations. I hadn't seen her in years, and the palpitations were caused by the Laura in my visions. I barely knew her. Why such distress? No, it wasn't distress. It was need, desire. I hadn't felt that strongly for any woman since Dossie Goldberg when I was seventeen. At least I got to touch Dossie Goldberg. But Laura Bishop was a whole different situation. She was a vision and a grown woman, beautiful in her blond allure. She was an out lesbian but somehow connected to Stratton. When she had looked at me in that trance-induced press conference, I could see her want for me matched mine for her. I was frightened and confused. I realized my thoughts were becoming jumbled and unfocused.

Tap, tap. I lifted my head from the steering wheel and looked to my left. The same female federal agent was watching me, her brows pinched together with concern. The gun on her belt somehow made me feel safe instead of evoking my usual horror fit over firearms.

"Are you okay, ma'am?" she asked.

I nodded and pointed to my belly. "Just a little sensitive stomach. I'll be better when I get on the road."

"Sorry about the delay. It was necessary, but you're free to leave now. Hope you feel better." She waved me forward. For a few crazy seconds, I didn't want to leave the ferry and the safety of that officer's gun. My headache ratcheted to a new level of agony.

❖

When I finally arrived at my condo, I unpacked, made some medicinal tea, and then sat in my study to call Fitch again. This time, she answered. Legal pad and pen at the ready, I asked what she had found out about Laura Bishop and, possibly, her connection to Elizabeth Stratton.

"They worked together," Fitch said, "at the local law firm of Meyers and Gaines. Except when Stratton was there, it was Meyers, Gaines, and Stratton. That was more than eight years ago. Stratton left the firm and her lucrative partnership to enter politics. She married the odious asshole Jerry Greenfield about the time she left her law practice.

"Maybe coincidentally, maybe not, Bishop left the firm about the same time. She then opened her own practice, Bishop and Associates. She's incredibly good at her work. Big cases, family law for the well-to-do of Seattle."

"Any idea why she left Meyers and Gaines?"

I could hear Fitch's keyboard clicking. "I entered, by a nifty back door, into their employee files." Knowing Fitch, she entered through a cyber crawl space rather than a back door. "Bishop had stellar reviews, and interestingly, all of them were signed by Stratton. Those files rightly predicted that Laura Bishop was on her way to being a crackerjack attorney."

"Any hints about their off-record relationship other than employee slash boss? Personal animosity with each other?" I was scribbling the information on the pad while I talked.

"Not from here, but I have ways to get to old e-mails. Want me to dig around?"

"Hmm, go ahead, but don't kill yourself doing it. When you have a little more on Bishop, focus on Stratton. I want to pay Laura Bishop a visit. Maybe she'll be willing to open up to me." I hoped Fitch didn't hear the nervous quaver in my voice.

"She's a babe, Dev. I wouldn't mind her opening up to me or my handcuffs."

"You shameless pervert." Fitch was pissing me off. The thought of her being with Laura in any intimate way made me clench my jaw. "Is there any information regarding her current love life?" Now I was being shameless.

"None, but I haven't looked deeply into her personal activities yet. I do know she comes from money, and both parents are alive but estranged from each other. The rest of her biography I'll turn to once I've started the search for archived Meyers and Gaines e-mails and any Stratton dirt."

"Perfect as always, Fitch old girl. And where does Laura Bishop live?"

"Her condo is located two blocks from your condo, for your stalking convenience."

"Aren't you funny." I wrote the pertinent information on my pad, thanked Fitch, and promised I'd call her when I learned more about the lovely and disturbing Laura Bishop. Finally, I asked Fitch to investigate the incident at the Smith Tower the previous evening. It was my priority question, but I felt reluctant to let Fitch know I cared about Laura.

Then I found a bottle of antacid medication, drank half of it, and wrote myself a reminder to call my acupuncturist in the morning. I was certain the stress was compromising my immune system.

❖

My sleeping herbs didn't help me that night. All the questions and information I was grappling with kept me tossing my bedcovers off and on. First, I would remember Senator Stratton's smooth, hypnotic voice asking me not to harm Laura Bishop, then I'd flip my blanket off. Then the High Priestess's voice would dismiss me as being somehow not enough. Not enough for what? I'd pull the blanket on. And then Pento mentioned "He-Who-Comes-Before" as if not knowing about this person were dangerous somehow. I flipped the blanket off. All these voices were mingled with Laura Bishop's scream as she fell from the tower. I pulled the blanket on. Finally, around three a.m., I huffed out of bed and went to my study. I needed to talk to somebody.

This time, instead of trying tarot card combinations, I simply sat in my office chair, rested my head on the chair back, and thought about all the questions that were plaguing my brain. I silently called to the High Priestess, asking her for an audience. Nothing happened.

My mind drifted to Elizabeth Stratton and her bizarre appearance at my isolated house in the San Juan Islands, and that made me pissed off. Who told her about me and my work? How did she find Tranquility? How dared she let her goons harass my friend; they even damaged Fitch's car. Stratton was a senator of the United States, a probable presidential candidate, and she was behaving like an underworld boss. My indignation caused me to grip the arms of the chair, so I attempted to relax my hands. My palms flattened and pushed onto something cold and hard. I opened my eyes and found myself on hands and knees, looking at a foot that was rocking a crescent moon. I was in front of the High Priestess, pressing my hands into the marble dais.

I took a deep breath, and as I looked to her face, another

realization came to me about this strange world I kept visiting: it had no smells. It was a vacuum, an absence of olfactory stimulation that left me unhinged, unable to use all my faculties in response to her or any of the other situations. Until that moment, I had never considered that the sense of smell was so crucial to human functioning.

"We only recreate the senses necessary for your ability to understand our designs for your services." Her eyes watched me from her immobile face.

"What is that supposed to mean?" I forced myself to stand and fought dizziness, feeling the weight of fatigue and anxiety.

"We believe the sense of smell is not necessary here, so we don't create olfactory experiences. Besides, we aren't adept at it. We've tried in the past, and our champions often became sick or overwhelmed. It's not necessary for our purposes anyway."

"Easy for you to say. I'm still unclear about your purposes or even if your purposes match mine. All I seem to get are harrowing experiences with no resolution and no questions answered."

"We can't directly tell you. That is an eternal rule of engagement between the Malignity and those who want to thwart it. You have been bred with the ability to find the answers you need and then rearrange events for a more... desirable outcome." Her lips barely moved when she spoke, but her eyes behind the frozen eyelids were active.

"I've been bred? What is that supposed to mean? What am I, a ranch animal?"

"Touch the pillar behind me. Utilize what you know."

Remembering the last time she, without moving, had pitched me against a pillar, I dragged my tired self behind the dais and touched the pillar, closing my eyes while doing so. I opened them to the rubble of the destroyed tower where I had last seen Laura Bishop.

Pento stood motionless next to a large stone that had once been part of the tower. I cleared my throat, knowing that would wake or activate him. I still wasn't sure what he was, so I settled on defining him as a benign, vaguely useful, robot spirit.

He turned toward me and jerked his arm aloft in greeting.

Before he could say anything, I said, "Where's Laura Bishop?" I twirled and ran around the tower debris, scanning for any sign of her. I knew she had been in the toppled tower. She had to be there. "Tell me where she is. Now."

"It changes every time you leave and return." He was shaking his helmeted head, acting as if I should have known how things worked in his *meshugana* Theater. "Surely you understand how it works now."

"No, I don't. Enlighten me, please."

"This is part of who you are, what you have been planned for. The lines have been established for countless millennia. They were established to balance the forces in your world and other worlds too. Our responsibility is to intervene when one line, in this case the Malignity line, gets too strong. We cannot enter your world, so we use other means to reach equilibrium."

"What do you mean by 'lines'? What is my role here?"

"Your role, the duty of your line, damsel, is to neutralize undue power of any other line. Look there." He pointed to a figure on a low hill about two hundred yards away.

"What's that got to do with lines?" I turned to find Pento gone again. "And what are 'lines' anyway?" I muttered as I started hiking, again in my slippers, across the synthetic terrain toward the whatever-it-was on the hill.

The familiar crunch and squeak of the "dirt" accompanied my ascent up the gradual hill. As I came closer, I was able to make out someone with a bowed head, looking at a table that was placed between him and me. I could see the glint of a few articles on the table, including a chalice. I was more intrigued by what looked like a dark red ribbon hanging straight down the front of the table.

I stopped for a moment, about a hundred feet from the table and the person whose head was still lowered. Once again, the inability to smell jarred me, and I felt ill-equipped to deal with whatever was coming at me. But I knew I'd need to confront this guy in order to continue on this bizarre quest.

"Hey, mister!" I called with an inadequate, flat voice.

Taking deliberate care and without lifting his head, he pointed to the ground with his right hand. Then he hiked up his left arm and pointed to the sky. I was looking at a tableau of the first major arcana tarot card, the Magician. He symbolized what a magician always is, a person who makes fantasy a reality, turns falsehoods into truths. An illusionist, a liar.

"Before the High Priestess comes the Magician. He-Who-Comes-Before," I said softly. Then he raised his head and looked at me. A warped grin smeared his greenish face. A face so malevolent I couldn't breathe. The red ribbon I'd noticed hanging from the front of the table originated from his hideous, perverted mouth. The ribbon streamed from his purple lips, off his chin, to the tabletop, then over the front side. The inch-wide red stream was trickling over the ground toward me. It was no ribbon. It was blood. And it was pooling at my feet.

I screamed and looked up at the Magician. His hair was the exact pompadour hair I'd seen Jerry Greenfield sport on television and the one time I'd seen him in person. Anger and disgust burst from me, and against any impulse I had ever experienced before, I attacked.

I tore up the hill toward him wanting to rip his face off. The blood that had drizzled from his mouth soaked into my socks. The dirt gave way beneath me, and I fell onto my knees. I looked at my hands buried in the blood and found myself looking at the ceiling of my study. Pre-dawn light made the room gray and colorless. I loosened my hands from gripping my thighs.

"I am so stupid. Greenfield. Of course," I said to the moth that was helplessly batting the light fixture in the middle of the ceiling.

CHAPTER EIGHT

After that distressing trip to the Theater, I schlepped my drained body into bed for a few hours of unsatisfying sleep. When I awoke, it was midmorning on Tuesday, a banal time to start a serious, possibly deadly, mission, it seemed to me.

Sipping decaffeinated black coffee and cursing my lactose intolerance, I settled at my desk and pondered the situation I'd gotten myself into. This was far bigger than some aging movie star learning, from my visions, that his hairdresser was going public about the hair implants. It was not like a derailment of a bodyguard who boffs the starlet in the limo and then threatens to release videos to the tabloids. Those kinds of events were easy to pre-empt.

Being conscripted by the High Priestess to avert some intangible disaster that I couldn't grasp was beyond my skill set. However, I had learned something crucial in my last trip to the Theater. I was given the unmistakable message the Magician gives all card readers when he points to the air and the ground simultaneously, the ancient alchemical message, "As above, so below."

What happened in the heavens also happened on earth. Spiritual and physical reality mirrored and informed each other. To focus on one side at the expense of the other was to dwell in extreme peril. From this, I concluded several things and castigated myself for being such a *schlemiel* for not having realized it right away.

I was developing an unproven hypothesis. The Theater was really that: a theater. I was its spectator. It was a place where the war in the alchemical world, or heavens if you like, was projected to me. A colossal multidimensional screen. Most likely, the cosmic energies involved used tarot symbolism because that was what I understood best. Were I a deep faith Christian, I'd probably see angels and devils locked in eternal combat. If I were immersed in Scandinavian mythology, I'd see Loki and Thor squabbling. The forces of good and evil, and those in between, engaged in an ancient battle for dominion. Dominion of what, I worried.

I knew I was in the middle of a cosmic and earthly game of tic-tac-toe. Not the one that you play with a friend on a scrap of paper while waiting to board an airplane. This was the tic-tac-toe played in three or more dimensions. Like the one with three levels and marbles, where so many contingencies have to be considered before making a move. A game where you are sure that you're missing something that will cause your sudden and mortifying defeat, and it's often true.

I poached an egg and slid it on top of a piece of toasted millet bread. When I finished eating, I had a plan for the day. I settled at my desk and grabbed the phone.

"Fitch, I thought I'd call you before I look for Laura Bishop and hear what you've dug up on her and the Smith Tower killings. Tell me what you know."

Fitch started relating information about Laura Bishop. "I have lots of information. She's a clean gal. No crimes, just a couple parking tickets. She is a lesbian who doesn't use online dating sites, but she does visit sites about lesbian culture. Her other frequented Internet sites center around lefty news, you know, like the Huff Post. No indication whether she has a girlfriend or not. haven't checked her shopping habits yet but I'll get to that. Her activities seem limited to numerous charities she supports and her pricey legal practice. A family law attorney and as good as they come. Lots of well-heeled clients but does her fair share of pro bono work for women and kids in shelters. Definitely not a tool of the extreme Christian right, anyway."

"Possible enemies?" My excursions to the Theater made it clear Laura Bishop was in danger, but from who and why? And what happened at Smith Tower, her office building, two days ago? I withstood my impatience and let Fitch deliver the information systematically.

Now Fitch's voice sobered a bit. "Lots of potential enemies. Family litigation dredges up the worst in people. Fighting over kids and property has become a bloody national sport. She has had her share of online death threats and a few through conventional mail and telephone calls. Fairly routine occurrences in her profession. Who knew? All threats were duly reported to the police and handled appropriately from what I can tell."

"No current or ongoing threats?" My mind kept rewinding and replaying the sight of Laura Bishop calling for help just before that tower fell.

"Here's where it gets interesting and where I deserve my reputation, Devy."

"Don't call me Devy. I'm not a Devy. Okay, prove once again what makes you the *macher* of cyberspace."

"I am the queen tuna of cyberspace because I know when to leave cyberspace and make a few phone calls. I thought Bishop would probably have some security, at least at her office, protecting her from the marauding ex-spouses she has litigated against. One call and I hit it big."

"Who did you call?"

"The manager of the security firm contracted by the Smith Tower is a long-standing, active member of the BDSM community. You should see her in vinyl, a sight for the ages. Anyway, she told me Smith Tower was vandalized last night, and the damage was located in Bishop's office. Here's the bad part."

"Let me guess. Three people were murdered, and it was Laura's office that was vandalized. Who was killed?" A crushing foreboding filled me as I imagined Laura Bishop lying dead in a marble hallway in the Smith Tower.

"Three security personnel had their throats slit. Cleanly. No struggle. Caught completely unawares. Whoever did the deed had been hiding in the building when it closed. All this is in today's papers, but there's more that didn't make the news." Three security personnel were dead, not Laura Bishop. I felt relief tinged with sadness for the poor guards who died just doing their jobs.

I focused again on Fitch. "Don't tell me what you had to promise to get this next bit."

Fitch was adept at trading use of her private dungeon for favors from people who liked to keep their kinks under wraps. Like the GLBT culture, there was an unseen BDSM culture that operated, unnoticed, under the noses of the average citizens. They supported each other's businesses and helped each other out when needed. I was beginning to think half of Seattle's couples kept sex torture toys in their bedside tables.

"Each guy had the letter *I* carved into his left cheek. Apparently done postmortem. But it gets more relevant and more off the record than that. Laura Bishop was there."

"Damn, why didn't you say so right away? Fitch, you know she's—"

"Wait, wait. She's okay. At least, she's in Harborview Hospital, unrevealed to the press, and doing fine. She just happened to stumble into the whole scene. Her office was being ransacked and she walked into it. She saw the guy. He threw something at her, knocked her out, and carved the same *I* into her cheek. Bishop had called nine-one-one before being attacked. The police tracked the cell phone signal. The attacker either thought she was dead and left, or he was scared off. Anyhow, he got away, but they think he's taken a ferry somewhere."

"Who got a look at him?" I knew it had to be Laura who helped the police artist make that drawing of the swastika skinhead.

"Bishop did. Big Nazi-looking dude. Buzzed hair. Gold-crowned tooth. A twisted cross tattoo on his neck. Sounds like one of the bastards that harassed me out on Lopez Island the other night while you were doing hoo-doo with Elizabeth Stratton. How much you want to bet he's the same guy?"

"Stratton again. What a *farshtinkener* day when I opened my door to that woman. I wonder if Laura Bishop was left for dead and they don't know she's alive and well at Harborview."

"We're talking Senator Elizabeth Stratton, wife of Jerry Greenfield, owners of a giant empire of bedroom snoops. If she doesn't know yet, she will soon enough, and Laura Bishop will be in big trouble. I had to dig, but I got all this information. No reason Stratton's toadies won't do the same."

"I'm going to see Bishop. Any idea what room she's in, or am I pushing my luck with your skills?"

"She's in room 445 West. Getting that piece of information is child's play. But just so you know, it's a secure wing. Good luck getting in."

"I have my trade secrets too, Fitch. Dig around on Stratton. We need more."

"Already in process. I'll call later."

When I hung up, instead of jumping into action and going to Laura Bishop, I sat for several minutes and pondered the agreement I'd made with Elizabeth Stratton. I'd never dishonored an agreement with a client, never even questioned the moral ramifications of my meddling. It was a winning formula, one that made me wealthy. Was there any reason to change? Was Elizabeth Stratton any more of a hypocrite than my other clients? Oh yeah, she was. In fact, Stratton and her Elmer Gantry of a husband were worse. They wanted to control the whole country. No, they wanted to control people.

And there I sat, a skinny Jewish girl who, science would claim, was experiencing psychotic hallucinations telling her to save the world. Regardless, all the years of studying paranormal phenomena helped me to trust my experiences with the High Priestess, Pento, and the Theater. To my core, I knew what was happening to me was real.

But who was I to take this on? Why me? Why now? Then I remembered the famous quote from Rabbi Hillel: "If I am not for myself, then who will be for me? And if I am only for myself, then what am I? And if not now, when?" For the first time in my life, I was doing something noble.

"Go figure," I said.

Several years ago, I conducted a reading with a client who was a nurse at Harborview Hospital. I had a vision that she would be busted for drug use in the near future. She gazed at me, shocked, as I relayed the image of handcuffs wrapping her wrists and she being wedged into a police cruiser.

"Actually, it's not me using drugs," she said. "It's my boyfriend. I…I steal drugs from the hospital for him to sell. I don't dare stop. He'd hurt me. You have no idea."

I told her that I certainly did have an idea about what kind of trouble her boyfriend was. I offered my services to send her boyfriend in another direction and get him out of her life. She was broke, having given all her money to, of course, the boyfriend. I wasn't above a convenient barter.

I knew men like that piece-of-dreck boyfriend were essentially cowards. He had his girlfriend do his dirty work, lived off her paycheck, and beat her to boot. He was a spineless loser. So I offered the pitiable nurse a trade. She would owe me some favors for a few years, and I'd redirect the boyfriend. I would get my own form of hospital privileges, and the boyfriend would ditch town when served with a convincing, yet phony, threat from the local underworld. Spotless, nobody hurt. It was that grateful nurse who smuggled me into Laura Bishop's hospital wing.

After my nurse friend got me into the secure hospital wing, she left me to find my way to Laura's room. I made it to the nurse's station of Laura's floor only to be stymied by Harborview's version of Big Nurse.

"But I'm Laura Bishop's girlfriend. Her...her partner. I have hospital privileges in the state of Washington." My palms were sweating in anticipation of finally coming face-to-face with Laura. Lying about being her partner didn't faze me.

"Her partner was already here. Dropped off her stuff and left a few minutes ago. You're not her because you don't have red hair. Besides, I can tell you're from a newspaper or something. You got that pushy East Coast accent." This woman had her meager mind made up. It was clear she wasn't going to let me past the security guard that stood by Laura's room door. I wasn't about to enlighten her about her prejudices for people from the East Coast.

Laura had a partner. I was irked at my twinge of disappointment. I was there to save her, not ask her on a date.

"Okay, but she knows me." At least I hoped she'd remember me. "She knows I can help her." I took one of my business cards from my wallet and grabbed a pen from the counter of the nurse's station. On the back of the card, I wrote, *Let me help you.*

"Please, give her this card. Can you promise to give her this card? Honest, I'm a friend. Please?"

Big Nurse took the card, studied both sides, and said, "You're not no ambulance chaser, are you?"

"Me? Oh, no. Besides, Ms. Bishop is an important Seattle attorney. She has her own people she can call. Can you give her the card? Please? She will appreciate it. I'm sure of that." I couldn't remember ever groveling as much as I did to that woman, not even to Rabbi Metzger when I was attending Hebrew school.

"Okay, but you gotta leave now. If Ms. Bishop wants to see you, she can call you, and then tell me that you're coming. You go away, and if she wants you, you'll hear later today. She's got hours of tests that start in a few minutes." She pointed to the elevator and waited while I got on and rode the elevator car to the lobby.

I needed time to think and unwind from being so close to Laura Bishop and then thwarted. An hour later, I was lying on my acupuncturist's table with twenty needles in my back, resembling a balding porcupine. I buried my face into the massage table face hole built specially for making patients comfortable while someone stuck several sadistic-looking needles into sensitive parts of the body. There was nothing like an acupuncture session to relax my body and clear my thought apparatus and digestive tract. However, on this day, nothing could calm me or my digestive tract. I thought about Laura Bishop and the danger she was in and considered her connection to Elizabeth Stratton.

Stratton. Who was she? What kind of game was she playing with people? Was she anything more than a demigod, feeding on people's fears? Her whole shtick was manufactured and infuriating. Painting herself as "any woman" when she was anything but. She was rich, extremely well educated, intelligent, and, according to my intuition, a faux Christian. In short, she was nothing like the snookered people who worshipped her for being just like them.

I was churning myself into an indignant lather when I heard the familiar, scratchy laugh of the High Priestess. Once again, I found myself on my hands and knees in front of her throne and gaping at her wooden-like foot. I looked up and saw that this time she had her ancient Torah open on her lap. This was not the traditional sheepskin, scrolled Torah Jews keep in synagogues. The High Priestess's version was bound in book form. In this case a bulky, worn leather tome with T-O-R-A-H spelled in worn gold lettering on the cover. She was riffling the pages with stiff, nail-less fingers. She didn't look at the book. Her unnerving eyes were watching me watch her fingers riffling the book. As the pages flipped by, bits of things, a mélange of cosmic *schmutz* were flying out of those pages. The bits looked like dried flower petals, matchbook covers, swizzle sticks, postcards, and other detritus from someone's vacation or senior prom. The items danced in the air around my face, tantalizing me, but I couldn't get a good look at them. I tried to capture the hypnotic bits, but they evaporated in my fingers.

I looked to the Priestess for an explanation but instead was looking at my acupuncturist's perplexed grin.

"You always fall asleep on the table, don't you? Don't

worry. It's a good sign. Means your body is responding to the needles. Something's shifted, though. All your needles were actually vibrating visibly this time. Big chi. Really big chi. Keep doing whatever it is you're doing, but be careful of wearing yourself out. Okay? I'll make you an herbal mixture to clear and balance the paths to your chakras." She plucked the needles out of me.

"Uh…sure…yeah…big chi." I twitched with each pluck.

Chapter Nine

I had just finished choking down the vile tea my acupuncturist concocted for my chakra alignment when my business line rang. The caller ID read "L. Bishop and Assoc." For a few endless seconds, I was so *fartootst*, I couldn't press the talk button. When I did, I choked out, "Devorah Rosten."

"This is Laura Bishop. I believe you were outside my room door this morning? I do remember our last meeting, Ms. Rosten, and was convinced we'd never cross paths again." She sounded weak physically, but her forthright, blunt approach reminded me she was an aggressively successful attorney.

"Yes, well, hello, Ms. Bishop. Look, I'm sorry to bother you, but I think we need to meet." The waver in my voice didn't make me sound like I had much help to offer her. Then I thought of something worse. I didn't have a plan.

"Your card said you could help me? Can you explain?" Her voice was melodic, exactly like I'd remembered, except with more maturity. This time, though, it was tinctured with an undertone of apprehension.

"If I explain in specifics, Ms. Bishop, it would take a long time. Plus, you might not believe me. But I need to ask you one question. Do you think you're in danger?"

I heard her take a deliberate deep breath and then bobble the phone. "Yes, I think it's possible that I'm in trouble. I don't want to involve anyone I know personally, for a variety of reasons. That's why I called you, Ms. Rosten."

"I'll do whatever I can. I think this situation is probably way bigger than the two of us. But in the meantime, you need help. Tell me what I can do." Again, I marveled at my impulsive willingness to help someone and not charge a fee. I was going to do something honorable, a mitzvah.

"I don't know where you learned that I was attacked, but I am injured. I need someone to discreetly handle a few things and help get me safely out of this hospital."

"Aren't the police protecting you? I saw the guard outside your room door."

"The guard will be removed tomorrow morning. I was told the city didn't have the budget to protect me longer than that since the police believe what happened at the Smith Tower was an isolated incident. They think I just happened to disturb a psychotic burglar who doesn't flinch at slitting throats of security guards."

"And what do you think, Ms. Bishop?"

"I think we need to get off the phone and get me out of here, but we have some things to do first. Will you help? It might be dangerous." Her voice caught on the word "dangerous."

"I'll help. Tell me what you need." I found a pencil and pushed a piece of paper in front of me to take notes.

"When I hang up, I'm going to immediately put you on my hospital next of kin roster. After that, I'll call the security office in my condo building. I want them to let you into my apartment, so bring some identification."

"Bring ID. Got it. Okay, where's your condo, and what do you want me to get?" I wasn't about to tell her I already had her condo address, a remnant of Fitch's snooping. Instead of supplying a list of items as I had expected, she gave me directions to one specific thing in her apartment. I wrote them on the scratch pad.

"Put it in a bag you'll find in the closet of my study. Get out of there and get to the hospital. The place may be watched, but since you are a stranger to my social circle, nobody will think you have anything to do with me." I heard someone come into Laura's room.

Laura's voice changed into a more conversational tone. "Oh, someone's here to change my dressing. I'd better go, hon. We'll see you later? And I'll make that call I promised in ten minutes, when my owie is all fixed up again. 'Kay?"

Even though nobody could hear me, I adopted the same breezy tone. "Yeah, sure. I'll wait around and see you in a little bit. Take care and don't worry."

While I waited to go to Laura's building, I took a handful of vitamin B, figuring it was the kind of support I'd need. Then I made sure my guest room was dusted and towels placed appropriately in the guest bathroom. I checked my hair, making sure it didn't look like the wrath of God. I changed into my most fetching black T-shirt, so that I'd look attractive and fit for a mission. Just before I walked out the door, I texted Fitch and reminded her to call me as soon as she had more information about Elizabeth Stratton. I should have heard from Fitch by then and wondered what held her up.

Laura's condo building was similar to mine. It was a Seattle Belltown neighborhood development for the upwardly mobile employees of Seattle corporations. Her building was sure to have solid security, a swimming pool, workout room, underground parking, and views priced according to how much of Elliott Bay was visible and how far one would plummet if exiting via the window.

Paradoxically, while living in our neighborhood was pricey, the riffraff of Seattle found the same streets welcoming. I knew the neighborhood association would change that soon, but in the meantime, everyone on the street looked like a thug because it was late in the evening. In short, I didn't feel comfortable until the muscular security guy let me in and showed me to the elevator.

The condo wasn't large, but it was lovely with art pieces that were both edgy and bold. Laura Bishop supported the arts. I liked that and wondered how she would feel about my hundreds of shelves of metaphysical and natural healing books housed mostly at Tranquility. I had some high-quality art at Tranquility, but I didn't have it in the quantity that Laura had.

The study was where she had described it. Behind the desk and to the right stood a bookcase with shelves designed for oversized books. On the shelves were perhaps a few dozen scrapbooks visibly brimming with memorabilia from Laura's life. An odd hobby for a woman of such accomplishment. It must have served some special purpose for her, and I wasn't about to psychoanalyze Laura Bishop before I'd even spent time with her.

Each scrapbook had a different binding both in texture and color. I found the light green leather volume that Laura had directed me to and eased it off the shelf. I set it on the desk and gently turned some of the stiffened pages. I recalled my most recent visit to the High Priestess and her Torah with debris flying out of it. I was on the right track. For once, I felt abreast of the High Priestess's game.

Needing to move quickly, I didn't really inspect the contents of the scrapbook. I simply noted it was full of the kind of tchotchkes a person collects to remember events.

Matchbooks, swizzle sticks, olive picks, bar coasters, receipts, tickets, and other paper items I was too hurried to inspect. I had no idea what the sum of these parts meant, but I trusted I'd find out soon enough.

I stuffed the scrapbook into an empty computer pack I found in the study's closet and hoisted the pack onto my back. I shut off the few lights I'd turned on except the one in the hallway, just like Laura had requested. I locked the door behind me.

When I left the building, I turned north toward my building and parking garage where I aimed to get my car and go to Harborview Hospital and Laura. Halfway down the block I was waylaid by an inebriated and shop-worn woman who wanted to show me her underpants in exchange for five dollars. She had an iron grip on the strap of the computer pack.

"I don't care if you're a girl, honey," she slurred inches from my face, "'cause girls like my undies too." Her breath was a fog of cheap whiskey.

"Look, lady, I'm not interested in your undies at all." She was no fool. She knew she was grossing me out, and I'd pay the five dollars just to get away from her. I dug in my pocket and came out with two ones. That seemed to appease her because she backed against the wall and folded her rear to the sidewalk. She didn't even look up at me, just sat there holding the two dollars as if she forgot she had them.

Embarrassed, I glanced down the block at the entrance to Laura's building to see if the security guard was witness to my humiliation. But he was busy talking to some big guy who looked fairly intimidating. I recalled Fitch's description of the guy who attacked Laura Bishop: "a big Nazi-looking dude." If anybody was a big Nazi-looking dude, it was that guy. Given the legacy of my people, anytime the word "Nazi" comes up, we clear out. And that's what I did.

❖

Getting on Laura's next of kin roster was like becoming a VIP at Harborview. I had no idea what Laura said to them, but it was effective because at eleven o'clock at night, I was shown to room 445 without any Big Nurse giving me grief.

Laura's eyes were closed when I entered the room, so I took a minute and watched her doze. The bandage on her head was fresh and seemed to focus on the side of her head, just above the ear. Another bandage covered where I assumed she'd had the capital *I* carved into her cheek. That bandage was smaller and less dramatic looking. The room lights softened the multihued bruises on her cheek that were flooding from under the bandage. Laura's wrist was bundled in an Ace wrap that braced a temporary splint. The fingers protruding from the splint looked swollen and purplish. Battered and bandaged, she was still the most compelling woman I'd ever shared space with.

For the first time in my memory, I had a nearly irresistible desire to touch another human being. I wanted to stroke her pallid but certain face, caress her hair, and comfort her as a loved one would. I didn't really know her, but I belonged with her, in that room, at that moment. Of that I was certain.

"Did you get the scrapbook, Ms. Rosten?" she said, still keeping her eyes closed. Abruptly she opened them, peered at me, and my heart lurched into an erratic rhythm that felt diagnosable. "Well, did you get it or what?" She eased and huffed herself into a more upright position. "I'm sorry. I was abrupt and thankless. You've gone out of your way for a near stranger. Here, let me see if it's the right scrapbook."

Obviously she didn't return my bizarre girl-crush feelings. I didn't blame her. I suspected my being smitten with her was related to some temporary psychosis peculiar only to me. A real pity, I thought, but probably for the best given the dire situation she was in. She didn't need a distraction.

Wordlessly, I eased the pack off my back and placed it on the bed tray and wheeled the tray to hover over Laura's lap. She attempted to loosen the scrapbook clasps with her one functional hand but fumbled enough to draw my rapt attention from her face to her struggle with the clasps.

"Oh, sorry, let me help." Together we worked the bag open and every time our hands glanced off each other, my mortifying blush deepened. It brought me some relief to notice how her hand jerked slightly every time she touched me. She felt something anyway. Whether it was attraction or repulsion, I would learn eventually.

With my help, she carefully withdrew the scrapbook and placed it on the bed tray, and I tossed the bag into the closet.

"Perfect. It's the right book. I was worried you wouldn't be able to tell them apart. Could you go back to the closet and find my purse?" she said. "There's a little voice recorder in the side pocket. I'm going to need it."

I felt a silly glow of pride that I'd done well so far. However, she was nervous about me. She wouldn't look at my face. I was so overwhelmed at finally meeting her again that I couldn't think of what I could say or do to ease her anxiety. The situation reminded me of a lost dog I'd seen a few weeks earlier. I tried to call it to me and entice it with a piece of my sandwich. It just stood there with its tongue lolling, panting, but wouldn't come nearer. When I took one step too close to it, the poor dog ran off, and I didn't see it again. In that hospital room, I was afraid of stepping too close and scaring off Laura Bishop. So for the time being, following her directions was my best option for winning her trust.

"So, Ms. Rosten, are you really here to help me or just

acquire another client? I'm curious about why you want to help me. After all, we met fairly contentiously a long time ago, didn't we?"

"It was eight years ago. I'm not sure I can give you an exact answer as to why I'm here. Let's say I was, um, called to it." I handed her the recorder. "I…I think I can help you, or at least I want to try." I stood next to the bed but decided she would trust me more if I sat and didn't loom over her. I moved the inhospitable hospital chair closer to the bed, directly in her line of vision, and sat on the unyielding brown stuffed plastic. One spring was pushing into my left butt cheek, probably making me look off balance. "My profession is to fix things, situations, for people. I'm pretty good at it."

"I have to admit, your being here seems right, like we're supposed to do this. Why me, though?" Every word she shared with me was weighed and chosen carefully. This was the job interview of my life.

"If I told you the whole story, it would take a long time. I promise I will tell you everything, but I don't think we have much time. I know you're in danger. I know what happened at your office building—"

"My office building is only part of it. There's more, more that is much worse and far riskier. Are you sure you want to be here, Ms. Rosten, because you are in danger while you're with me. This shattered wrist, concussion, and the face carving are fruits of this danger."

My stomach heaved at her words, but I attempted to hide my apprehension. "I know you're in danger and a little about why. Together, we can work out this situation. I have lots of resources and connections. Plus, in some sense, I'm compelled to help you." My voice sounded nearly brave. But what did I know from heroics?

"Ms. Rosten, the reason I called you is because I didn't want to involve friends and loved ones in a chaos of my own creation. You are a neutral party, and I need that neutrality for what I want to do. Can you remain unbiased for the next few hours?" She touched the bandage on her head, reminding me that the danger was genuine.

"Please call me Dev. I'm not sure if I am unbiased or neutral, even right now, but I can be nonjudgmental. My clients tell me things, secrets, that I'll carry to the grave rather than divulge them. It's my line of work to know the secrets. Tell me why you're in trouble, Laura. May I call you Laura?"

She nodded as if making a decision about something more important than what we would call each other. "Yes, call me Laura, and you are witness to what I'm going to tell you. That's where the recorder comes in. And the scrapbook. All this is for testimony, evidence. I need proof and witnesses. I forgot to tell you to bring a camera. Does your cell phone have a decent camera?"

I pulled my phone out of my pants pocket, checked the battery, and said, "It's a great camera, top of the line, and we have a full battery."

She was gazing at me as if seeing me, really seeing me, for the first time. I felt vulnerable. "Good," she said. "There will be a few pages in this scrapbook that I'll want you to photograph as I proceed." She was wincing occasionally from pain, but her voice was solid and sure. If she was going to give me the whole story, she needed to be as lucid as possible and was resisting her medication in order to do so. "I've been under heavy pain medication. If anything I say is unclear or out of sequence, stop me and ask questions. Can you do that?"

"Of course, anything you need. Would you like more water before you begin?" She gestured toward her glass with the bent straw, and I filled it from the plastic pitcher left by the sink. "Can you operate the recorder with your good hand? Or would you like my help with that?"

"It's voice activated, so it won't be a problem. Get comfortable in the chair. I'll let you know when I need pictures snapped." I faked comfort in the chair. She clicked the recorder and began.

"Eleven years ago, when I was twenty-seven, I was a freshly minted attorney. I landed a dream job at Meyers, Gaines, and Stratton here in Seattle. Elizabeth Stratton was one of the founding partners of the firm. Several months after starting as an associate, I received a memo from Elizabeth asking me to meet her for lunch. Here's the memo. Photograph it, please." I took the first of what would end up being dozens of pictures that evening.

Her face was determined. Her measured pace of speech hinted that she had rehearsed this story before I'd gotten there. "From that lunch where she presented my exemplary professional evaluation, we became friends of sorts. Almost daily, she would stop by my office and chat for a few minutes. She'd send me an occasional humorous e-mail, like this one here."

She pointed to one of those e-mails like everyone receives, the kind that contains several jokes. The jokes pasted on the scrapbook page were all derogatory about attorneys. At the top, Stratton had typed, "Makes you proud to go to work every day."

"Photograph it?" I asked.

She thought for a moment. "Not yet, there are meatier things to come," she said and turned the page. The next few pages contained mementoes from bars and restaurants: napkins with tavern names, fancy promotional matchbooks, after-dinner mint wrappers, and a few receipts. She had me photograph the receipts, making sure the dates were clearly visible in the picture.

"Elizabeth and I were meeting socially once a week eventually. At that time, she wasn't what she is today. She was an aggressive attorney, sure, but she was warm, funny, and compassionate. She was never dogmatic. I was young, but even if I met that past Elizabeth today, I would never predict the self-serving monster she's become."

"So what happened to change her?" I was baffled by the Elizabeth Stratton that Laura described.

"Let's deconstruct her after I finish my story. Then you'll have more information to formulate your theories. By the way, I've never told anyone what I'm going to tell you. I ask you to keep the same confidentiality that you keep for your clients." The IV tube that was plugged in the back of her hand trembled a little now. She was weak. We couldn't keep this up all night. I looked at the clock. It was nearing midnight.

"If I weren't discreet, I would be out of business." That statement nudged the question that had nagged me all night. Should I tell Laura that I was hired by Stratton to derail her? I made the decision to wait. I had no idea what would change if I told her, but I didn't want her to send me away.

She turned the page of the scrapbook. Even that small effort cost her. She was pale and needed rest, but she continued. "All the receipts on this page are from Manzanita, Oregon. If you notice, you'll see that they have different dates stretching over a period of two years."

Some were faded, but I could see they were from the period of Laura's employment at Meyers, Gaines, and Stratton. Most were from restaurants, and she'd pasted them in chronological order.

"Elizabeth and I began our affair at a luxury beach house the firm owned in Manzanita." She was looking at me, not at the page. She was gauging my reaction. I've sat in the face of hundreds of sordid revelations from my clients, but this was one I hadn't expected. I didn't cover my surprise well.

"What surprises you the most, Dev? That a religious icon could have a lesbian relationship or that I'd get into bed with a blatant hypocrite?" The annoyance she felt lifted one of the eyebrows on that intelligent forehead, and her eyes lasered on me.

I squirmed on the chair spring that was torturing my left butt cheek. "Laura, you have to admit, a claim that Senator Elizabeth Stratton, presidential candidate, and wife of Reverend Jerry Greenfield, had a two-year lesbian relationship is, well, a surprise. Not a shock, just a surprise. You are making allegations about a person who sponsors and votes for more anti-gay initiatives than just about any member of the federal government."

"I can assure you of two things. I am not making up any of this, and Elizabeth Stratton is not the straight woman everyone believes her to be. Would you like me to detail our sexual encounters?" Her right eyelid was quivering from either exhaustion or emotion. "Because, trust me, in the hundreds of times we had sex, Elizabeth was not only an extremely willing participant, she was the enthusiastic initiator."

I nodded. "That she was the initiator, I can believe. A detailed description of you two having sex? No thank you." The thought of Laura Bishop having sex with anyone, never mind Elizabeth Stratton, made me heartsick. I was losing any objectivity where Laura was concerned. "Tell me the other parts of this story."

Laura looked at the scrapbook and turned a page. "Here, on this page and the next several pages, are all her love notes. Some came with flowers or stuffed animals that would be sitting on my office desk when I'd arrive in the morning. They were unsigned, of course, but Elizabeth's handwriting is distinctive. Some love letters came via regular mail. Those were the most torrid, again, unsigned but in her handwriting. She kept our work e-mail clean of any hint of our relationship, just jokes or interesting quotes came on my work computer. Take a picture of each of these love notes, please."

Grateful to be distracted from the thought of Laura's body entwined with Stratton's, I took several pictures of the love notes and cards. I even moved a table lamp closer to the bed to help sharpen the pictures. While I was busy snapping photographs, Laura trudged on with her story.

"Of course, being young and still a little naïve, I had dreams that Elizabeth would conquer her discomfort with going public with our relationship. I dreamed that she would agree to come to my home for dinner or that we could lie in bed all morning at her house and make love. But that never happened. We always met in local hotels or spent weekends in Manzanita." Laura's voice was growing weaker, and I started to wonder if she would hold up much longer.

"Tell me how it ended, Laura, and why it ended." I had put my folded jacket on the seat of the chair, making it a tiny bit more tolerable to sit there.

She settled back into her bed pillows and gazed at the wall at the end of the room. "When I think back on it, Elizabeth's withdrawal from me started six months before the very end. More and more days separated our meet-ups. She would claim being busy with one thing or another. But when we were together, she was just as passionate, almost desperately so. There was a clinging need in her that hadn't existed before. I mistook it for her being ready to commit. In fact, now I know she knew we'd be ending, and she wanted to get what she could before...before it was over." A tear ran down her wan cheek.

I had to ask. "Do you still love her, Laura?"

"Love her? No, not in that way. But I cry for that younger Laura and that lost Elizabeth. I was unable to state what I wanted from her and fight for it. She was unable to overcome her ambition and fear. We were always doomed, right from the start. It still hurts, though."

I had experienced a few hurts in my time and could only offer a few hollow words to Laura. "Of course, the hurt of a breakup never really goes away, I think. It just digs deeper into our hearts where it hides under layers of scar tissue. Sometimes we scrape at the scar tissue, and the hurt peeks out to remind us of what we lost." I reached over and carefully took her IV-punctured hand in mine. "Tell me the rest."

She glanced at our joined hands then at me. Finally she rested her eyes on the scrapbook. "One day, I was sitting in my office and heard a commotion of delight in the reception area. I peeked out my door and saw the Reverend Jerry Greenfield and a couple other polished suits parading around the secretaries, giving the women schoolgirl vapors. Elizabeth was watching the scene with a bewildering show of satisfaction." Laura paused for several moments to gather strength and to stem more tears.

Jerry Greenfield, I thought, the Magician, the manipulator. "Was that the first time you had ever seen the two of them together?"

"It was, although I knew Elizabeth had done some legal work for his mega-church in Kirkland. I hadn't put them together even as acquaintances. I assumed she'd just met with his representatives. He was already a national hero for the religious right by then."

"Elizabeth didn't express any qualms about representing someone like Greenfield?" I couldn't imagine any attorney wanting to represent a snake, but then I supposed there were attorneys who were snakes themselves.

"The one conversation we had about it was brief and defensive. She said he was only protecting his rights, and she was compelled, as one of his attorneys, to fight for him. She was clear the topic was off the discussion table." Laura sighed, loosed my hand, and started picking at the bandage wrapping the splint on her left wrist.

"Tell me the rest, Laura. We need it on tape."

"Well, that day was pretty much it. Elizabeth and I were never lovers again. She cut me off without explanation, without fanfare. No note, no fond good-bye, no fuck you. A couple months later, she sent word in an official memo that we had to meet for lunch at a downtown Mexican restaurant to discuss my future with the firm." Laura's face had hardened, and the trails of her tears had dried, leaving a line of salty residue on the cheek that was bandaged.

"She fired you because you two had been *shtupping* for two years?" I was growing angrier with every new angle of the story.

Laura's eyes flashed at me. "Hey, I don't need a translation for that one."

"The beauty of Yiddish. Sounds like what it is. Sorry if I sounded coarse. Tell me about that lunch."

"Well, she didn't fire me. Quite the opposite, in fact. She told me she was leaving the firm and offered her lucrative caseload to me. She said I could handle it better than any of the other associates. And, yes, it felt like a buy-off, not an accolade."

"What did you tell her? Did you take on her caseload?"

"I resigned from Meyers, Gaines, and Stratton. I gave her my two-week notice, a fairly unprofessional thing to do in the legal world, but I had some pride. I told her that she'd better come across with great references for me, or she'd find herself in court with a giant, public sexual harassment suit to deal with." By the set of Laura's jaw, it was clear that she had re-empowered herself during that lunch. "Afterward, Elizabeth wrote glowing references for me. I'm proud to say they were accurate, not trumped up. Several months later, she announced both her candidacy for Washington state senator and her engagement to Jerry Greenfield."

"How were you doing during all that?" My heart was in pain for her.

"I was crushed, but I felt oddly strong, even emboldened. That's when my friend Margaret gifted me with that reading with you." Her small smile at me was tinged with a little guilt. "Sorry I was such a pill. Your reading was more accurate than I wanted to believe. I started my own law practice, and it grew steadily. Elizabeth even referred a few clients to me. A sort of peace offering, I hoped, but was probably meant to keep me quiet. And I was quiet. Until now."

"And now you feel you have to say something."

"As of yesterday, yes, to expose who she really is. Back when Elizabeth and I were in the throes of our passion, it didn't feel like *shtupping* or whatever. For a time, she loved me. I know it. It was the real thing. I'm sure most people have relationships they regret but know the emotions were real at the time. Well, that one was mine. But now other people are paying for it. The American people need to know what Elizabeth is." She was agitated, and it brought a little color into her face.

"How do you mean 'other people are paying for it'?" As if I had to ask.

"Those murdered security guards. It was no coincidence that it was my suite that was burgled. My office is on the twenty-third floor, for God's sake. No burglar would ride an elevator to the twenty-third floor and then randomly decide to ransack one attorney's office suite. Not when there are twenty-two floors beneath that are faster to get to and house offices containing far more expensive items than mine."

"What are the police saying about that? Surely they understand your reasoning." I was in agreement with Laura but wanted to learn one more thing.

"The police are turning a deaf ear to whatever I say to them. I'm beginning to suspect the worst."

"And that is—"

"The police are somehow beholden to Jerry Greenfield and Senator Stratton. Because I'm sure that guy who killed the security guards did so because the guards caught him on their cameras. Somehow, the murderer dispatched those three poor men, then went to my office to see if there was any damaging information about Elizabeth. Information that could affect her chances of running for president."

I looked at the scrapbook still open in front of her. The scrapbook was exactly what the killer was looking for. And it was sitting right in front of us. There were still several pages to discuss, and Laura's energy was slipping away from her. Her injuries, compounded by the emotions the scrapbook unearthed, were taking their toll.

"Let's continue through the rest of the book. What does it contain?" I reached to turn the page. Laura rested her hand on my forearm. I loved the feel of it there. She seemed to note the effect of our touching and moved her hand onto the scrapbook.

"There's nothing more of importance in there. Just clippings recording Elizabeth's rise from attorney, to senator, her marriage, and her plans to run for president. Nothing more to look at." She closed the scrapbook and left her hand on the cover, as if protecting it from my prying. She didn't leave me any time to wonder about that. "We have to get me out of here. They won't stop at killing innocent security guards. I have to go somewhere they won't suspect, with someone they've never associated me with." She looked into my eyes. "I'm hoping that someone will be you, Dev."

She had me, and somehow, she knew it. I was helpless to turn her down. Something between us was shifting. We both felt it, but in her injured state, I'm sure our nascent attraction was more confusing for her than it was for me. "Helping you is why I'm here."

There were other things that were troubling me. Confessing my recent meeting with Elizabeth Stratton was only one of my conundrums. I was also worried about how I'd handle the two of them simultaneously. Was that possible to do safely? I shook off my confusion and concentrated on our immediate situation. "What do you have in mind?"

"I have to get past that guard out there. Then we need to hide the scrapbook somewhere while we figure out what to do." She was fidgeting with her IV tube, then she held up her hand and looked at me expectantly.

I backed away and shook my head. "What…what do you want me to do?"

She was grinning a little, an adorable little grin. "C'mon, you can do it, Dev. Millions of people pull out IVs every day. It can't be too hard, can it?'

"But I'm not a medical professional. I'm a third grade school teacher turned tarot reader. Blood upsets me." I had backed myself into the wall and was considering hiding myself in the closet until she got the needle out herself.

"Well, you can't expect me to do it. It's too personal. The sight of my own blood makes me faint, and I'm already in a weakened state." Her face took on a pleading look that I knew had the capacity to rule my life. "Please, Dev? You're the only one who can do this for me." She lifted her hand a little higher.

"Gevalt," I said and stepped to the bed. "I hope you're ready to help me off the floor when I keel over."

"You won't keel. Just study which direction it enters my hand and pull it out in the opposite direction. How hard can it be?"

"Yeah, but I can't forget that it's in your vein. And your vein contains blood. Lots of blood." Nevertheless, I cupped her right hand in my left and studied the needle. Despite the stress of the moment, I was thrilled to have her hand in mine. Carefully, I peeled off the tape that held the needle in place. I looked into her face, and despite the bandages, she appeared open and receptive to me. Trusting even. I couldn't let her down.

I calmed my panicked breathing, took a firm hold of the needle with my thumb and forefinger, and said, "Are you ready for this?"

"Yes," she said and looked at the wall.

I started silently counting my breaths. One. Two. Three, and I jerked the needle away from her hand.

"Ow!" she squeaked. "That hurt. That hurt way more than it should have." We looked at the back of her hand. Blood oozed over it, but it wasn't spurting. For that, I was thankful. "Get that towel over there, and wrap my hand in it. Ow. Shit."

I wrapped the towel around her hand. "Be sure to press on the puncture. That will stop the bleeding." That was as much as I knew about first aid.

"Damn, that hurt. Not your fault, though." She was rocking over her cradled hand.

I glanced at the door, worried a nurse would enter to investigate our noise, but we must have been quiet enough.

"Look, we have to get you dressed. Did your partner bring you any clean clothes?"

"My partner? I don't have— Wait, you must be talking about Margaret. She brought my clothes."

"Earlier today the nurse told me your partner had been here. Said she had red hair."

"Margaret is my best friend. We have an agreement. If either one of us lands in the hospital, we claim the other one is her partner. We trust each other to make decisions, plus, neither one of us wants our parents to come swooping in. That would be an even worse fate."

"So you have no partner?" I was embarrassed by the hope in my voice.

She eyed me for a moment then smiled, "Uh, no S.O. at the present." Her smile disappeared, and she was back to the seriousness of our situation. "Margaret left a bag of clothes in the closet. Get it out for me, would you?"

A gym bag rested on the floor of the closet. I retrieved it and placed it on her bed.

She stared at the bag's zipper because her cast on one hand and the towel wrapped around the other made it impossible for her to manage.

"Oh, let me do that." I worked the reluctant zipper open and fished around in the bag. I pulled out a pair of sweats, a warm hoodie, T-shirt, socks, sneakers, and then I coughed.

She looked at what I was holding. "Do you collect anything, Dev?"

"Uh, sure, I collect mystical books and artifacts. Why?" I was still looking at the items in my hands: an ensemble of silk underpants and bra that must have set Laura back at least five hundred dollars.

"Well, besides scrapbooks, I collect lingerie. Put the bra

back, please. I can't manage it tonight, and I'm not about to ask for help with that."

That was disappointing and a relief at the same time. "Right, nobody should put on a bra at two a.m.," I said and regretted saying it. "Can you manage the rest? I'll turn around and give you space."

"Fine. Be patient. This will take a while. I'm still a little woozy. A lot woozy, actually." Her bedclothes rustled. She groaned a few times, but I kept my back turned. Laura Bishop seemed to be the kind of woman who only asked for help when things were dire. "It's my shoes," she said with an impatient huff. "I just can't manage them."

I whisked around the bed, squatted down, wedged her socked feet into the sneakers, and tied the laces. When I stood, our faces were too close. Without thinking, I touched the bandage on her cheek. It had a small fleck of blood seeping through. I inspected it and decided it was not fresh, so the I carved into her cheek wasn't still bleeding. "I'm sorry this happened to you, Laura. So sorry."

For a moment, her face crumpled, revealing both grief and fear. The moment passed almost as soon as it started. She drew herself up and looked into my eyes.

"Thank you. Thank you for, well, everything." Her eyes were tearing. She didn't put her hands on me, but she leaned her head into my shoulder as if to gain strength and comfort. Then she straightened. "How do we get past that guard? Any ideas?"

"Yeah, actually, I have an idea. Get back into bed and cover up to your neck. Look tired, asleep even."

"That won't be hard," she said and crawled under the covers.

I waited by the room door until she was in position and

nodded at me. I made a silent wave and opened the door so the guard could see Laura. "Okay, Ms. Bishop," I said, trying to keep my voice relaxed. "I'll inform everyone at the office that we'll start back to work on Thursday. Good thing too. This late working session has taken a toll on both of us."

"Good night, then," Laura said in an exhausted voice.

I shut the door and looked at the police officer guarding her room. He was well equipped with a gun and club hitched to his belt.

"She's the manic boss from hell," I said. "She makes me work here till all hours of the morning just to close the office for a few days." I noticed the shadows under the officer's eyes. "I bet you feel the same way about your higher-ups, huh?"

"Got that right, lady. But it's my job to protect and serve, so here I sit." The coffee in his Styrofoam cup had long ago stopped steaming and was even leaving a ring on the inside. A testament to its vile taste and age.

"Well, thanks for the work, Officer. Hopefully, we won't see each other again."

He chuckled, lifted his bent cup to me, and said, "I'll drink to that." He took a sip and winced.

I laughed. "Please don't. That's above and beyond the call." I walked to the elevator, pressed the down button, and waited. When the elevator door opened, I stepped inside, watched the door close, and took a peek at the police officer who had already forgotten about me. I rode the elevator to the lobby level, stepped out, allowed the door to close behind me, and waited again. Then I pressed the up button, got back on the next elevator, and rode back to Laura's floor.

When the door opened, I rushed to the officer, who had his eyes closed and head leaning against the wall. "Officer, pardon me for bothering you again." I infused my voice with more than a hint of breathy panic.

"What is it, lady? You worked so late you can't remember where you put your car?" He grinned at me.

"Oh gosh, no. I wish that were the case. There were two guys. Downstairs. In the lobby. They got on the elevator."

"Uh-huh. And you need to tell me this, why?" Perfect, he was getting annoyed.

"Well, they had shaved heads. They looked kinda like the guy that attacked my boss, Ms. Bishop." He was watching me closely now.

"Explain, ma'am."

"They were just...creepy. I can't explain it, but I know bad news when I see it, Officer." I was enjoying the bimbo tone of voice I was using. He appeared to respond to the helpless girly act. "They had scary tattoos too. And they got in the elevator next to mine. I don't know what floor they went to, but they looked like trouble to me. Do you think you could check them out? I don't want to leave until I know Ms. Bishop is completely safe. I'm a loyal employee, you know."

"I'm sure you are, ma'am. But I shouldn't leave this hallway." He had already set his cup of caffeine swill on the floor and now stood.

"I'll stay right here. And if a nurse comes by, I'll get her to stick around too. Okay? Please? Just check for me, or I'll never get any sleep tonight." I was happy nobody saw me bat my eyes at him. It was a mortifying moment.

"Okay, I'll check the next few floors down. That's about how long I can stay away from my post. If anything happens, yell...loud. Got it?"

"Loud. Yeah, I got it." I plopped myself into his chair and watched him race to the stairs. I didn't expect that. I had assumed he'd use the elevator.

"Oh crap." I stepped to Laura's door, pushed it open to find her waiting right next to it, her shoulder propped against the wall. "Let's move. Quick." I kept my arm around her waist as we scurried to the elevator. The stairs were out as an escape route.

I pressed the down button then scanned Laura's body. "Where's the scrapbook and voice recorder?"

"I thought you had them," she said.

"Shit. Wait here. Hold the door when it opens."

"Oh, grab my bag too. The orange one in the closet. It has my wallet."

I ran back to her room, grabbed the scrapbook and recorder off the bed table, and dumped them in the backpack I'd carried the scrapbook in initially. I found her orange cloth bag in the closet. I ran back to the elevator. Laura was waiting inside, so weakened she could barely hold the door open.

"Press P-Three, Laura. That's where I'm parked."

She pressed the proper button then leaned into the elevator wall. Her face was ashen. "I haven't taken any oral painkillers, so when the stuff in my veins wears off, I'll be in deep trouble."

"Don't worry. I've got a veritable cornucopia of goodies in my medicine cabinet. Nothing as good as the intravenous stuff, but it will take the edge off. We need you less drugged anyhow." I moved next to her and again wrapped my arm around her waist. She leaned into me. It felt right. We rode the rest of the way down in silence.

When the elevator door slid open, I held my hand up to forestall Laura. Edging my head out the door, I scanned the parking garage for signs of movement. My dark blue Lexus was parked only a few spaces from the elevator, so it wouldn't take but a moment to reach the car. The garage looked deserted except for a few lone vehicles. Most of the spaces were empty.

"Okay, it looks safe," I said. "Let's move to that blue

Lexus over there." We walked quickly to my car while casting looks around to check for anyone following us.

"That cop is going to go all batshit when he finds out I've left, Dev. That will be any minute now," Laura said as we settled into the car.

"Worry not. We'll be out of here in a few more minutes." I started the car and eased out of the parking space. As we moved up through the next few floors, we didn't see any movement. Given it was almost three a.m., that wasn't surprising. The poor shmoe who worked the ticket booth when I paid to exit the garage only wanted to get back to his iPod and graphic novel. He barely looked at us.

The quiet Lexus took us down First Hill to downtown Seattle. The dripping streets were deserted with the exception of the building doorways being used as sleeping dorms for the city's homeless population. I thought about the woman I'd encountered earlier outside Laura's building and hoped the two dollars I'd given her to avoid seeing her underwear had bought her some solace that wet night. Probably not.

"Why a scrapbook, Laura?"

She jumped at the sound of my voice. She'd already been dozing off. "What? I don't get your question." Her voice had grown gruff with fatigue.

"Why did you put all those things chronicling your relationship with Stratton into a scrapbook? I saw dozens of other scrapbooks on your bookshelf when I went to get the Stratton one. I know you collect underwear, but that's not the only thing you collect, is it?"

She laid her head back on the seat. "No, it's not. My other hobby, besides reading about the law, is scrapbooking. I've been doing it since I was a kid." She was holding her splinted arm, and I knew she was in pain. I wanted to take her mind off it.

"So what made you pick up that kind of hobby? You don't strike me as a particularly nostalgic person."

"Why? Because I'm an overpriced attorney? A spoiled rich kid? A lesbian?" I assumed her testy defensiveness was drug and pain induced, so I continued.

"Well, yeah, maybe because of all those reasons. Tell me why you keep things in scrapbooks. I'm interested." I kept my eyes on the road. Every time I came to an intersection, I'd check the rain-soaked, empty streets for skinheads. She was doing the same thing.

"It was my nanny, Vesta. My parents hired her so they wouldn't have to bother with me. That way they could fight and have more cognac. That was their particular favorite hobby: drinking cognac and verbally torturing each other. Vesta had gotten proficient at removing me from my parents' sparring ring. One day, their fighting was more heated than usual. Vesta took me to my room where I cried and begged her to take me out of that house. Talk about a gilded cage." She grew quiet with the memories.

"And the scrapbooking?"

"Oh, yeah. Sorry." She took a deep breath. "Vesta soothed me that day in a way I didn't expect. She pulled out a book, a scrapbook. Then she produced a box, the kind a large pair of boots came in. Inside that box were mementoes she had saved for me. Things like report cards, holiday cards, birthday party favors, pictures of friends, all kinds of things. When I saw what she had saved in that box, I knew she loved me. It was a feeling, a dawning of awareness that I'll never forget."

She was quiet for a few moments while more tears drizzled her cheeks. "Anyhow, Vesta said I should take up a hobby and record all my great moments, my friends, my victories, and such. She had all the glue and tape along with a colorful book that was all about the hobby of scrapbooking. I must have been about nine years old, and I've been scrapbooking ever since. It's a balm for my heart when things are hard."

"Where's Vesta now?" I was driving into the garage of my condo building in Belltown.

"She died a couple years ago. Alzheimer's. I had her in a wonderful care facility here in Seattle, but she slipped away from me." Lines of deep sadness furrowed her face.

"What about your parents? Are they still around?"

"I know you're just trying to keep my mind off my physical pain, Dev, but you're not helping my emotions. And my parents live on opposite coasts, as far away from each other as they can get. It works well for all three of us." She saw I had parked the car. "Can we go upstairs now? I'm so tired and I hurt."

"Absolutely, but we need to check the halls as we go. I don't think they know about me yet, but it's just a matter of time." I got out and pulled the pack holding the scrapbook out of the backseat. I went around to her door and opened it. "Ready?"

She looked up at me for a long moment. Her gaze made my heart do a flitter. "Well, I'm ready. Are you ready, Devorah Rosten?"

The number of allusions in that question kept me stumped for a few seconds. "Yeah, Laura Bishop, I'm ready. We'll figure this out together."

She took my hand while holding her injured wrist close to her body. We encountered nothing untoward while en route to my condo. Once we were inside, I knew we were safe, but only for the time being.

CHAPTER TEN

L aura went to my bathroom to visit my medicine cabinet. I heard a soft "Oh my God," after she turned the light on. I wasn't sure if she was impressed by my extensive pharmacopeia or by my decadent bathroom. I went to the bathroom door to see what had wowed her. She was looking at my Jacuzzi.

"Can I use that?" She sounded breathless with longing.

"Of course, but first I'll have to put a plastic bag over your wrist, okay?" She nodded. "Look in the medicine cabinets to the far right. You'll find a whole shelf of pain medication. And don't ask how I got them." I had a couple of pharmacist clients always willing to keep my cabinet stocked. "I'll get you a big glass of water so you can take your pill. Don't feel like you need to drink bathroom water. Yuck." I left the bathroom avoiding the quizzical look on her face.

When I returned with the plastic bag, a rubber band, and a tall glass of water, Laura already had the tub filling. Steam rose from the stream of hot water crashing into the deep tub.

"Can you handle all this yourself? Do you need help covering your wrist?"

"No, I think I can manage. This tub is heaven-sent. I just want to be in it." She was watching the water cascade from the faucet. Her face looked both exhausted and dreamy.

"Well, try not to fall asleep in there, or I'll need to come haul you out."

She cast a lazy wicked look at me. "Would that be so terrible?"

"Uh, right now, yes. We have to get out of town as soon as possible. Then we can make a plan. Okay?"

"Okay. Go away now." She turned back to watch the water.

I put the glass of water on the vanity next to the plastic bag and rubber band. "That's a new loofah there, so help yourself." I closed the door of the steaming bathroom behind me and headed to my study, as far away from Laura Bishop as I could go within the condo. I forced myself not to think of her naked in my bathroom. Instead, I sank into my desk chair and brooded about my situation.

What was I going to tell Laura about my visions? My clients thought I could only see possible futures for them. As far as I knew, only Fitch knew that my tarot trances had taken a wild turn into the freakish Theater with Laura Bishop making harrowing cameo appearances. Fitch could bend with the bizarre, but Laura? I didn't think so.

I paced my office and wrung my hands while Laura bathed, naked of all things, in my bathroom of all places.

"Underwear." I muttered a few times as I paced. "She likes underwear. My perfect little life is perfectly doomed."

The time was rolling into four a.m., but I needed a live distraction. I fished my cell phone from my pocket and speed-dialed Fitch.

"I know," she said, "I'm the only person you can call at this hour who won't be pissed off at you. But I am a little annoyed, just not at you. This Stratton thing is testing my skills, and winning, so far." I could hear Fitch *schlump* herself into a chair and start clicking on her keyboard. I had a passing thought that a clicking keyboard was the soundtrack of Fitch's life. Then I thought of her dungeon, and dropped the keyboard soundtrack thought.

"It's uncanny, Devy, I can't find anything on Stratton."

"I'm not a Devy. What do you mean 'can't find anything on Stratton'?" I realized I was speaking loudly and lowered my voice in case Laura was done with her bath and within hearing distance. "Stratton should be easy. She's a public figure. Her biography is an open book, isn't it?" I continued to pace.

"One would think, but it's no open book. At least no open book with appendix or footnotes. Her history definitely starts at late childhood in Boulder, Colorado. Any further back from then, it's murky."

"Her parents?"

"Deceased. Killed in a car accident when Stratton was eight years old. No immediate relatives, so she's raised by a family friend. A nondescript schoolteacher who died when Stratton was twenty-one. Stratton has no surviving family that's traceable."

"Any school or medical records?"

"Well, yeah, they were easy to find. Too easy. They popped right up with barely a hack, like they were put there for me or anyone else to find. And then they are cursory, as if to hide other things."

"So what do they say?"

"Good grades, sound health, nothing interesting. No teacher notes or comments. No comments by doctors, not even a prescription. Nothing personal, like most of the narrative of her young life was painted over, leaving nothing to capture anyone's attention. In short, it's too boring. And I don't think a dynamic character like Stratton would have a colorless childhood. I think all this information is a plant, a screen to keep the researcher from collecting the facts about Stratton.

It's a testament to the laziness of the media that nobody has tried to dig deeper. They just accept what's supplied."

"What about college and law school? Anything there?" I lay down on the office couch and kicked my shoes off over the arm.

"A little bit more, but still only an outline of a life. She skied in college, but everyone does that in Colorado, don't they? She was a member of the Alpha Gamma Delta sorority, but only barely. She's not portrayed as an active member. She's in only one of their yearbook pictures, and it looks like she never even lived in the sorority house. She was a member of a pre-law club where she was a little more active but not gung-ho. It was in law school where she became visible, but all those activities are part of her bio. I don't have any reason to doubt them, but I do have reason to doubt the completeness of her official biography."

"What about her relationships, the ones before her *shmegegge* husband? Any pictures from sorority formals or other sorts of activities. Because I just learned that she and Laura Bishop had a two-year affair." I told her Laura's story and how it was all chronicled in the scrapbook.

Fitch started chuckling, an evil gotcha kind of chuckle. "Oh, now you're talking. Some red meat for old Fitch to sniff out. Pegging Stratton as a lez just made my job easier because I was looking for male attractions. And I wondered why there were no signs of any girl-boy relationships. She's a looker, so I imagine she attracted some attention from those randy mountain lesbians, but if she ever reciprocated, I can't find it yet. And I do mean 'yet,' because now they have the Fitch on the trail. Something is hinky here, and I'm determined to find out more. It's going to take more than me hacking in everywhere. I have to go to ground."

"What do you mean?"

"Get my hands dirty. I'll close my dungeon for a few days, make phone calls, and travel to Colorado at least. The more information we can get on Stratton, the better."

"While you're there, look for other threads, not only about Stratton but about Greenfield. I suspect they share some history, some commonality. Check it out, would you. Oh, and one more thing, there's more than Bishop is telling me. I just have a feeling she's leaving something out of her story. In short, be thorough."

"Anything to save our country from those two weasels. I'll call you when I find something, Devy."

"I'm not a Devy." But she had already hung up.

"Who are you talking to at this hour?" Laura had opened the door of the office and was standing there looking like she'd just stepped off the half-shell and donned my robe.

"I, uh, that was just my, uh, my research assistant."

"At this hour? Sure it wasn't your girlfriend or maybe a boyfriend?" She took a few steps into the room. She was holding a small tube of something that looked like it had come from my medicine cabinet. She had removed the hospital's bandage from her cheek and replaced it with two flesh-toned bandages. The spot on her skull that had been hit by the giant vase was covered by her hair only. The previous large wrap bandage was gone.

"Uh, no, no, there's nothing like that in my life. A girlfriend, that is. That's what I'd prefer if there were, um. Well, let's get the guest room ready for you, shall we?" For being a hospital escapee, she looked luscious, bruises and all. "We might as well catch some sleep until the banks open and we can store your evidence." I eased around her and walked into the hall, but she had me so *farmisht* that, in my confusion, I walked past the guest room. I recovered and turned around without losing face. "Oy, must be tired."

She followed me into the guest room and stood patiently while I avoided her eyes and turned down the bed. I fluffed her pillows, then turned to leave. She blocked my way to the door.

"Devorah, I need to thank you. I don't know what I could ever do to repay you for all this help."

Any truthful answer to that would have earned me a whack across the head, so I said, "It's my pleasure, and probably my mission. So get some sleep. We'll be up and going all too soon." I walked to the door and looked back. Her pallor was losing its post-bath pinkness, becoming sallow. "Did you find the pain medication in the cabinet?"

She nodded. "It should take hold in another half hour. In the meantime, I'm going to use up all your arnica cream on my cheek and a few other bruises I found on myself while I was bathing. That all right?"

"Please, help yourself to anything you need. I'll wake you in a few hours."

❖

I went back to my office, plugged in the heating pad, placed it on the small of my back, and stretched out on the couch. If I got into my comfortable bed, I would never wake up. And Laura's life depended upon me waking up and getting her out of there.

I thought about how weak but determined she was in that hospital room. We had created a convincing body of circumstantial evidence that Elizabeth Stratton could be involved with the deaths of the security guards and the attack on Laura. Eliminating Laura would eliminate a problem Stratton could face trying to become president. Her dewy-eyed constituents wouldn't want to vote for an ex-lesbian, would they? Would Stratton's affair with Laura really be that much of an impediment to the presidency?

Laura Bishop. Who was she? Some recipient of an embryonic do-gooder urge in me? My feelings about her were confusing. I had an inconvenient attraction for her, and that made this whole situation more complicated and frightening.

Stratton. She was my problem, and she was my client. She could destroy my career, or she could make me rich. When I followed that thought thread, however, I also had to accept that I was another one of Stratton's liabilities. If she could brutally have innocent people killed, all to further her sickening career, I would be just another piece of collateral damage for Stratton. That meant that Laura's scrapbook and the voice recorder were my life insurance.

I rolled on my side, attempting to make the couch feel at least partially comfortable. I propped the heating pad between me and the couch's back and pulled an afghan my mother crocheted over my chilled shoulders. I didn't savor the thought of what we had to do the next day. Every move we made could be dangerous. Laura was being hunted. I was certain of that. Anyone accompanying her was also prey to the hulking Nazi thug. I wished I knew who he was. Knowing something about him might help us protect ourselves. I should have sent Fitch on his trail too.

What really worried me was Elizabeth Stratton's power. She was a senator, so she probably had allies everywhere. She was also a hero to people who adulated her as God's messenger. A messenger with a manufactured biography, a bio as fabricated as the Theater that Pento created to send me his little messages.

The messages from the Theater were proving to be prescient. They had warned me of Laura's danger in the tower and the importance of the scrapbook. But what about the sword-wielding knight? Was that the skinhead who attacked Laura or the guy I saw outside her condo building? I assumed he was the same character, along with being one of the jackasses that harassed Fitch when she was on Lopez Island with me.

Or could that Knight of Swords be someone else? Stratton? Someone not yet identified? The tableau of Laura tied up on the beach was perverse in a way I couldn't understand. Her helplessness and vulnerability contrasted appallingly his unambiguous lack of mercy. Laura was not to be spared.

The few hours I'd spent with Laura Bishop turned something in me. I had a rare twinge of compassion for a client's target. I didn't pity Laura because she was so obviously capable. Her plan to use the scrapbook, voice recording, and photographs to expose Stratton was the best anyone could have done in her compromised situation. She was logical and determined. But if she made it off Lopez Island, where I planned to stash her, she could bring down the whole Elizabeth Stratton/Jerry Greenfield machine. My job, according to Stratton, was to stop her from doing that. Without Stratton's knowledge, though, I was going to make sure Laura wasn't hurt.

I measured, balanced, weighed, even sniffed any idea that could help me achieve Elizabeth Stratton's aims and keep Laura safe. And I still had to decipher why I was going to the Theater and what I was supposed to learn there. What did the High Priestess and Pento expect me to do?

I was getting more frustrated as I discarded one idea after another. Stratton's desire for power was really a mockery of our political system; worse, it was a mockery of the deluded people who believed in her. They gave her their money, time, and their integrity, like little children who kowtow to the popular kid on the playground. Anger began to seethe through me. I huffed and turned the other way on the couch, pinching my eyes closed to force sleep.

"Does your head have an ache, damsel?" Pento's clipped speech made me open my eyes to find myself lying atop a hill overlooking the synthetic ocean of the Theater. A few birds fluttered overhead, but they looked more like rubber Halloween bats.

"Hey, I just realized something, Pento. It doesn't hurt as much to visit you anymore. Why is that?" I turned onto my back and looked up at him. I was becoming used to seeing him from that angle.

"I rebuilt the portal. I am sorry, damsel. I had built it too narrow. An old habit from a long time ago. Humans used to be smaller." His mostly inanimate face didn't project much remorse. "But happily I have fixed your ache of the head problem."

"Yeah, at least that much in my life has been fixed. Not that I asked to come here in the first place." I hiked myself to standing and peered out at the ocean. Staring at Pento's too-smooth face made me uneasy. "What are those things on the water? Are they boats?"

"Oh, yes. Do you not recognize where you are? Look around."

I looked to my right. One long staff was staked into the ground. To my left were two more. Me standing on the hill with the staffs, the ocean with boats all added up to the tarot card the Three of Wands: trade, commerce, but what else? Discovery? Self-discovery? My prodigious knowledge of the cards wasn't working. Dizziness washed over me, and I grabbed one of the wands for support, making myself part of the card's tableau.

"Nice arrangement, Pento, but I don't see what this has to do with my real problems." My socks were collecting bits of the "dirt" that Pento had created. "Why me? Why tarot? You and the High Priestess act as if I should understand everything that happens to me here."

"You are learning who you are. You are of the line. You are who we must communicate with, and you are the intermediary. This is your destiny, your fulfillment. Without you, the Malignity gains strength. It already has in too many parts of the human world. You are the expert at hindering as you were planned to be. Now you are being called upon because we cannot go where you can. And we cannot give you specific instructions, so we use what you know."

"I think I've already figured that last part out. For some cosmic reason you can't give me direct orders, just hints. Why? Why not tell me to go redirect someone specifically? I do it, and we're all happy."

"You know the rules of earth learning, damsel. Choice. For you humans, in your world, all the lessons are about choice. For us in the Theater we must offer, maybe suggest, choices without interfering. We prefer certain choices over others so that the Malignity does not get too strong or too weak, for that matter. There must be balance. Look there." Pento pointed behind me, away from the ocean view. Desperate human wailing and keening assailed the air. I felt like maggots squiggled over my skin.

About fifty feet away, two people were turned away from me. They were dressed in rags; their bowed, heaving backs projected utter misery. Their cries and whimpers were of heart-wrenching loss. Far to my left slid a smirking little man. He was clad in rich brocade that was sewn with silver thread glinting in the light of the Theater's sun. He was confiscating five large swords, pleased with himself for being the source of such devastation. The scene was permeated with gothic grief and terror.

"The Five of Swords. Degradation, infamy, and dishonor in all their forms," I whispered while I watched the dispiriting scene melt away and disappear, leaving only the imitation dirt and weeds for me to gaze at. "So you are telling me the loss of choice brings sorrow, the Malignity, to humans? Is that what you want me to understand? And does this have anything to do with Laura Bishop and Elizabeth Stratton?"

"As you say, damsel," Pento said from behind me.

"What does that mean? 'As you say'?" I turned to him but, as was now his habit, he'd disappeared. "You're a coward, Pento. Can't you ignore your asinine rules and give me some answers? We are running out of time here."

I had turned around and started down the hill toward the ocean when someone grabbed my shoulder from behind. I spun around, and my face was six inches from Laura Bishop's.

"It's time to get going, Dev." Her voice was singsong and muted. We were in my office. I was still on the couch and she was fully dressed in her sweats and shoes. Her silken hair hung loose around her shoulders. Her breath smelled like toothpaste. Instead of moving away, her face, her lips, actually, moved closer to mine and gave me the lightest peck. "That was to wake you up and out of that dream. Did you know you mumble in your sleep?"

Before I could answer, she was heading out the office door saying, "I made coffee. Want some?"

"Uh, did you brew the decaf?"

"Not on your life," she hollered from down the hall.

CHAPTER ELEVEN

Before we left for Tranquility, we had to do something with the scrapbook and voice recorder. I called my bank and reserved a safe deposit box at the branch I planned to take us to. I decided to keep my phone with the photographs with me, but I wasn't so generous with Laura.

We were standing before Laura's opened orange bag where it sat on the kitchen counter. "They'll be watching your bank branches, not mine. In fact, from now on, all our expenses go on my credit card. Your credit card transactions are probably being traced. And give me your phone." I took the memory card out of Laura's phone and broke it in half before Laura could figure out what was happening.

"What about all my contacts? My apps?" Laura was livid. I supposed so much of her identity had already been assailed. She couldn't abide one more indignity.

"All those are replaceable. You, however, are not. Your phone is a giant beacon sent to how many satellites we'll never know. Sorry, but it's unavoidable. We can't afford to underestimate Stratton's power. She could have this traced." I scissored the SIM card into miniscule pieces.

"I think breaking it in half did the trick." Laura watched me dump the twenty teeny pieces of SIM card into the garbage. "Do you think you're a little obsessive sometimes?"

I threw Laura a glance. "Not any more than someone who collects tchochkes and uses them to record her whole life in scrapbooks." I rinsed my coffee cup and left in the sink.

"Touché, I guess." Laura clonked her un-rinsed cup next to mine. "Shall we go to your bank then?"

"First, let me make a few calls to get my house on Lopez Island ready for us. I want to make sure it's safe there before Stratton's minions figure out we're together." I gathered our few travel bags and some water bottles from the refrigerator.

Laura was fidgeting as if she couldn't wait to get moving. "Why would they suspect us being together? We only came in contact last night, and I don't think anyone saw us together, except maybe a nurse's aide who had no idea who you are."

"Those kinds of people have ways." I interrupted myself when I noticed Laura was watching me with mounting anxiety and some distrust. "Oh, hey…really, I'm here for you. I'm committed to doing what it takes to get you out of this safely. Can you believe that?"

She weighed my words. "I will for now. But if you aren't what you say you are, a friend, then I'll have your butt in court when all of this is over. When I'm through with you, you'll be sitting on the street out there trying, without success, to peddle pencils. Okay?"

Her show of force delighted me. She was feeling better. "Whoa, now I see why you're a hotshot attorney. Even with the bandage and cast, you've morphed into Mighty Ms. Litigation."

"I want you on notice, that's all. I don't like doing the intimidating attorney thing, but I can do it when necessary." She winced and cradled her wrist. "I need another of your codeine pills. I'm only taking half a dose because I don't want to be knocked out. I have a feeling I'm going to need all my faculties today." She removed the bottle of codeine from her orange bag and helped herself to one.

I waited until she had swallowed her pill and downed a glass of water. I stepped toward her, and grabbed her hand. "Okay, Laura, I'm on notice. But you don't have to threaten me. I've got a safe place to go and other resources. We'll get this whole thing worked out so that both of us are satisfied."

"What do you mean 'both of us are satisfied'?" Her voice had softened and she looked into my eyes with a tiny glimmer of trust.

I dropped her hand and moved back. "Uh, well, I mean safe. We'll be safe. Let's go."

❖

Depositing the scrapbook and voice recorder in a safe deposit box at my bank downtown was uneventful. When we were free of the items, we both remarked at how much better it felt to have them off our hands and in a safe place. Then we took a downtown exit to I-5 north and headed to Anacortes. We were aiming for the ferry that would take us to Lopez Island and our final destination, Tranquility.

The ninety-minute drive gave us an opportunity to talk to each other like two grown-ups who weren't trying to escape precarious circumstances. Laura was especially interested in my profession.

"Is it a religion with you?" Laura asked.

"Religion? No, I'm Jewish, remember? No, it's not a religion, it's a technology." Laura gave a disbelieving tsk. "It is. It's a method of contacting the wisdom of the unconscious and something else."

"Something else?"

"The Others. Those who live outside this realm but care about it…tend it, I guess. They are willing to send information, but only in the language of symbols and numbers. It's up to the reader of cards to interpret them. Some readers are better than others, but frankly, I'm the best." I knew that sounded arrogant. It was arrogant, but it was the truth.

She was shaking her head. "Look, Dev, you have to understand the world I come from. I traffic in logical arguments built from an enormous volume of words. I spend my days arranging and interpreting words to win legal battles. There is no room for something like tarot. It's too squishy for me, not concrete enough. You can't expect me to understand, nor accept, that access to the other side of existence is possible via a pack of cards comprised of symbols and numbers. The one time I was your client was a gift to me from Margaret. It didn't mean I bought your paradigm."

I understood her argument, but I wanted to make my point. "And you think the manipulation of words is not squishy? Isn't legalese just another form of symbols and numbers?"

A light rain had started and covered the windows in shimmering vertical streaks. The patter on the car was soothing. Both of us remained silent for a few minutes to absorb each other's viewpoints.

I glanced at her, taking my eyes off the road for a few seconds. I expected her eyes to project derision for my profession. Instead, she was watching me with a fondness that fluttered my heart. "Why are you looking at me like that?" I was getting uneasy under her gaze.

"Well, you have to admit, you are nice to look at. With enough exotic in your looks to make you more than interesting. But that's not all. I'm impressed with your bravery."

"My what?" This was going in a direction I hadn't prepared for.

"Bravery." She turned more fully toward me. "Look at what I've become. An attorney. A safe and respectable profession. But you, you've taken on work that's controversial at best. It's edgy. You don't even have 'Tarot Reader' on your business cards because it's not something everyone understands. But that's what you are."

"There are plenty of professional tarot readers who are up front about what they do. They don't have the enhanced services that I offer. I'm the only one. I can afford to be more discreet about my work." I worried about the direction the rest of the conversation would take.

"Aren't you worried about the ethics of what you do?" There it was, the scorching conundrum about my work.

"To tell the truth, sometimes I am. Other times, it's clear that I'm helping someone who really needs and deserves my help. And lately it's been made clear to me that I'm doing what I was meant to do, no matter how problematic the ethics." That was the first time I'd acknowledged what Pento had been telling me. I was born to be a meddler, and my meddling was even sanctioned by those in charge, whoever they were.

Laura turned and faced the highway again. "I'm feeling a little woozy. I think I'll lay my head back and close my eyes for a few minutes. That okay with you?" She pushed the button on the side of her seat, and it hummed her into a more prone position.

"You relax. We'll be at the ferry in another forty-five minutes." I was glad she needed to rest. I needed to think without her distracting me.

I was in a mental snarl. I had discussed some aspects of my work with Laura, but I didn't tell her about the Theater, Pento, or the High Priestess. Somehow, it didn't feel appropriate yet. What was worse, though, was that I didn't say a word about my connection to Elizabeth Stratton. That was a piece of information I didn't want to share, not only because of the $125,000 check still in the drawer at Tranquility, but because I didn't want to lose Laura's trust. I was beginning to feel her trust was more important than any promise I'd made Stratton. So how could I manage Stratton and retain Laura's belief in me? She'd said I was brave. Nobody had ever said that about me. I didn't want to disillusion her. She was beginning to mean something to me. That was dangerous.

I pondered the meeting I'd had with Stratton only a few days previously. She didn't seem threatening, not in the physical sense anyway. However, her people were running a rampage on Laura. My guess is they were out of Stratton's control. Maybe they were answering to Jerry Greenfield, because I couldn't see a presidential contender using blatant thugs to win the office. That would be dynamite in the hands of her political foes. No, Stratton hadn't hired the skinheads.

My guess was whoever had hired the cutthroats had lost control of them. Trying to kill an old lesbian lover was way over the top. It didn't warrant murder. Discrediting anything Laura said was an effective political response that would quell the Stratton as lesbian questions. Then what did warrant murder? What was I missing?

I looked at Laura sleeping in the seat next to me. Her mouth barely open, facial muscles relaxed, golden hair spread against the headrest. What do you know, Laura Bishop, I thought. What are you not telling me?

I was puzzling over all that when we pulled into the ferry line. I woke Laura, who sat up and fiddled with her arm splint for a moment. She didn't say a word as we sat in the car while waiting in the boarding line. When the ferry personnel finally directed our car to its parking spot aboard the ferry, I turned off the ignition. As soon as I did, Laura reached across her casted hand and clutched mine.

"He's here," Laura said.

"What? Who?" My danger instinct ignited.

"The skinhead guy. The one in my office. I saw him. On the upper deck, but he wasn't looking at us. He was doing something with his phone." Laura was whispering.

I looked around. Nobody. "Get out of the car. Now." She didn't move; she just looked at me in hopeless fear. "Laura, you can't seize up on me. We have to be a team or we're in big trouble. Grab your purse. Are the pain pills in there?" She nodded. "Good, we might have to abandon the car. But I can get us help on the other side if we need it."

"What are we going to do?"

"Well, they know we're together. They possibly know about my house on Lopez." Guilt nagged me because I hadn't told her Stratton had already been to Tranquility, escorted by the marauding skinheads who terrorized Fitch. "I hope they don't know how much I invested in security there. I have a priceless collection of mystical items, from books to goblets to amulets. They're of great value to some collectors. I'm a collector too, and my collection is extensive and well-guarded."

The other drivers and passengers were leaving their cars to climb to the upper decks and enjoy their scenic ferry ride to the San Juan Islands. The fragrance of ocean and car fumes filled our car. The plum bruise on Laura's cheek looked like it was impossibly darker under the bandage.

"So we have to become a part of your collection. Guarded and scared," Laura said. "I don't like it, Dev. Being trapped on an island. We should just go back to Seattle, get the scrapbook and tape recorder, and call the press. It's the only safe way out."

"No!" My adamancy surprised her. "I mean, listen, there's more…uh."

"More? What?" The grip of her hand on my arm was probably leaving marks.

"Hey, let go. That hurts. Okay?" She loosened her grasp on my arm. "There has to be more that they're afraid of. Something you have will expose more than Stratton's affair with you. I'm beginning to think Stratton might be a puppet, whether she knows it or not. And they are extremely invested in keeping her under their control. And part of that is information control."

Laura was panting from her mounting fear. It wasn't clear to me if she could hear what I was saying. I had to calm her, or we'd never get out of that ferry alive.

"Laura, look at me. Look. At. Me." She forced herself to look into my eyes, and I forced myself not to project the lava of fear that was coursing through me. "If we stay calm and focused, we can get out of here safely. I need for you to follow me. I know this ferry. I ride it all the time. That's our advantage along with this." I reached under my seat and pulled out the tire iron I'd hidden there earlier. I hadn't wanted Laura to know I was preparing for danger. Besides, if I had told her about the tire iron, my fear would be as obvious as hers. One frightened chicken is annoying; two frightened chickens will topple the henhouse.

Laura nodded and worked at controlling her breathing. "What should we do?"

"I'll put the iron up my sleeve. Then we'll exit the car and do the one thing he will least expect."

"And that is?" Her voice shook.

"We'll go after him."

"And do what?" She was squeezing my wrist again.

"I…I guess we'll have to take him out." When I saw her astonished face, I said, "I don't mean kill him, exactly, I guess. We'll just incapacitate him somehow. Laura, he's the guy who attacked you. You saw him, remember? You have every right now to protect yourself. Don't get all doubtful here. We have to go for it."

"Okay, okay. Your logic makes sense, sort of. But first I think we need to isolate him, you know, so it doesn't look like we attacked him." Now she was getting into it. She had no idea how relieved I was to have her agreement. I heard the bubbling rumble of the engines and felt the ferry sway as it left the dock.

We made our plan within a few minutes. Given the lack of time to think things through, I'm sure Laura felt as unconfident as I did. But we both crawled out of the car like a couple of cocky butches that we weren't. We wound our way through the empty cars to the stairway. The wind tunneling through the car deck carried enough sea chill that we were grateful to open the weighty door leading to the warmer upper decks.

Washington State ferries were built as a series of decks. Each deck sat atop the other and diminished in size the higher the deck, like a cigar-shaped wedding cake. The bottom two decks held vehicles that varied in size from semi-truck to bicycles. The bicycles and motorcycles rode at the very front on the lowest deck. It was a wonderful view from there but usually too windy and frigid for anyone to stay there long.

Above the two vehicle decks were the two decks where passengers lounged after leaving their cars. There was always a cafeteria or food vending area on one of those decks. They also held the restrooms and outdoor promenades where people enjoyed the fresh air. A semi-protected smoking area allowed smokers to, theoretically, avoid offending the clean-air breathers.

Laura and I attempted to act casually. Never mind that she looked like a war casualty and I had a tire iron stiffening my left arm. In fact, we were so noticeable that all the passengers pretended they weren't staring at us. We edged into one of the empty booths that lined the outside walls of the largest passenger cabin and sat opposite each other.

"See him?" I asked in a lowered voice.

"Not yet, but everyone else sees us. That can't be good," Laura said mimicking my voice level. She rested her casted wrist on the table in front of us. I noticed her thumb had lost most of its swelling.

"If they can see us, they can see him. We're safe right here. Let's wait a little longer until we're closer to the Islands. It's a short ride." I had no idea why I suggested that and apparently, Laura didn't either.

"I don't think I can wait." She was almost whispering now. "I'll go crazy if we do. Let's just take a moment and think over our plan again, see if it still holds. Okay?"

I nodded and thought about the plan while scanning the room. We no longer interested anybody. Everyone was busy fiddling with phones and cameras. One boothful of passengers had a deck of cards and cribbage board. A few booths were occupied by twentysomethings with their backpacks. Their tanned, strong bodies nestled down for naps because gorgeous scenery meant nothing at their age. Getting to the destination while listening to their entire music library was their goal.

Just as I was convinced that nobody was paying attention to us, I saw him. He had positioned himself toward the front of the ferry, his back toward us. Like other passengers, he was occupied with what looked like a cell phone. He was a walking cliché. His bulk filled the army green T-shirt so that the sleeves wrapped tightly around his solid biceps. He even had camouflage fatigues of the desert variety. His head was shaved, except a two-inch band down the center where a fuzz of blond was allowed to sprout.

I was sure anyone who noticed him thought he was a soldier on leave from one of the Middle East entanglements. For all they knew, he was a hero. That bought him clueless allies. We really did need to isolate him.

"He's behind you, Laura. Don't turn around. Just look out the window for a while and wait for the rest of the passengers to empty their bladders. He's playing with his cell phone. At least I hope that's what it is. Let's pray he won't detonate something even though he's on this boat. I don't think he's the martyr brigade type."

Laura's eyes widened. She started to touch the bandage on her cheek but stopped herself. "What makes you think he won't destroy all of us for his cause, whatever that is?"

"Two reasons. First, I suspect he's too valuable to his handlers. He's their golem, the monster they've created. Second, he wouldn't spend all those hours in the gym only to spatter his rock hard abs over the Strait of Juan de Fuca."

"Glad you feel so sure, but I don't. Plus, he probably isn't working alone. Where are the others? And there is one more thing I wanted to tell you. I think my pill popping is making my memory sluggish, but it started working as we climbed the stairs a few minutes ago. I think I know who that guy is. I just need to take one more glance at him to be sure. What's he doing now?" She sat up a little straighter.

"Looks like he's texting, not sure. I think you can look now. I'll count to three. Ready?" She nodded and I began counting. "One, two…not now. He's looking up." I closed my eyes as if dozing. The rumble from the ferry engines and the murmurs from other passengers were so mundane that, with my eyes closed, I could almost believe the world was normal again. When I opened my eyes, he was gone. "Shit. Laura, he's gone. We need to move. Now."

"Okay." She was taking deep breaths, cradling her broken wrist, and looking in my eyes. "We follow the plan?"

"Yeah, we follow the plan. Ready? Go."

I watched as she stood and said in a clear voice, "I need to go to the bathroom. Could you get me a cup of coffee?"

"Sure. I'll meet you back here. Cream or sugar?"

She looked at me like I'd lost my mind, then said, "Cream," and marched toward the restrooms.

I waited exactly one minute, then made my way to the cafeteria. The tire iron in my sleeve made me look disabled; I was sure of that. Using only my right hand, I poured the largest cup of steaming coffee that they sold from the dispenser. I skipped the cream and waited in an excruciating line before I paid for it without waiting for change. I walked toward the entrance to the women's bathroom. It had been about four and a half minutes since Laura and I split up.

When I paused outside the bathroom, I worked the tire iron into my pants so it stuck out of my waistband. I prayed it wouldn't fall down my pant leg before I had a chance to clobber someone. After I removed the lid to the coffee, I slid into the bathroom entrance grateful there was no heavy door to push open. A stall door banged so hard the wall shook. Turning the corner, I was faced with our stalker holding a knife under Laura's throat. She was bleeding where the blade touched her throat. Her terror-drenched eyes met mine in the mirror. The back of his neck was at least seven inches in diameter. A swastika tattoo peeked from under his T-shirt collar and was within my reach.

"What's up?" I tried to sound clueless. Before he could move, I pulled open the back of his T-shirt and poured the blazing-hot coffee down his bare back.

He barked once and threw Laura against the sink. The sight of her blood on the porcelain was all I needed. I jerked the tire iron out of my pants just as he turned to face me. I swung the tire iron at the brute. My blow glanced off his forehead. Enraged, he stepped toward me but didn't see the puddle of coffee on the floor. He lost his footing and crashed forward. While he was on his knees, I hit him again on the back of his muscle-dense neck. He wasn't out, but he was down.

I jerked the lever on the paper towel dispenser and ripped off a few lengths of towel. I handed the towel to Laura, grabbed her upper arm, and pulled her toward the bathroom door. "Cover your neck," I said. Then I went back and hit the back of the brute's head. The splat sound it made was revolting. I almost dropped the tire iron but remembered to hang on to it. I pushed it back into my pants, blood and all, and pulled my shirt over it.

"I'm bleeding," she gasped.

"I know. Let's get downstairs." I grabbed her purse off the floor. If she was walking, she was okay enough to get somewhere away from the wheezing assailant and all that blood collecting around his head. When we left the room, I vaguely noted the blended smell of blood and coffee and thought what a rare mixture that was.

There was no way Laura's color could have gotten whiter. Luckily, the restroom was located a few feet from the stairs that led to the car decks. We passed one startled mom and her kid on their way to the bathroom.

"They're out of order," I said to them. "Use the one on the other side." I hoped she didn't hear the hysteria in my voice. I also hoped she didn't know that there was no women's restroom on the other side. I just wanted them away from the danger and mess on that bathroom floor.

We stumbled down the stairs but stopped at the upper car deck. It was a ferry mezzanine harboring only cars. It overlooked the lower deck of vehicles that included cars, trucks of all sizes, and towed vehicles. My car was on the lower deck sandwiched between a pickup truck and an SUV towing a small speedboat. We could see the faint reflection off the sunroof of my car. From our vantage point, nobody was near it. In fact, there were no people moving on any of the upper or lower car decks. Either the passengers were enjoying ferry amenities, or they had stayed in their vehicles for privacy.

"Is it safe to go back to your car?" Laura was talking just loud enough for me to hear her over the engine rumble and blasting sea wind. Her hair was batting into my face, and I noticed that some of it was bloodied. I felt my cheek to find it was wet with Laura's blood.

"It's not safe anywhere on this boat. Let me look at your neck." I peeled the paper towel away from her throat and inspected the cut. "It's not that bad, really. It's already coagulating. We probably should get a bandage on it just to keep you from looking like you've been in a slasher film."

"I am in a slasher film. I...I don't think..." She started choking sobs.

"Hey, hey, now's not the time. I promise you can melt down all you want later. For now, we need to hide out and get ourselves to Tranquility." I was cupping her uninjured cheek. She looked into my eyes and I could physically sense her trust. I felt like a major *schlamozel*, a luckless loser. She was the most captivating woman I'd ever met, and it was my fate that she was my client's target.

"That guy wasn't dead, Dev. He's either going to blow the whistle on us or come after us, with vengeance as an added motive." She leaned her head into my hand.

"For the moment, he won't bother us. He's hurt and he's in a women's bathroom. The ferry personnel may suspect him of some perverted foul play. At least that's what I hope." I turned and peered at my car. He would look for us there if he were able-bodied, but we needed that car.

My watch read 1:05 p.m. We'd be at the Lopez dock in fifteen minutes. I glanced at Laura and found her slumping over the railing. She needed rest and probably something for pain.

"It won't be long now, Laura. Can you make it down one more flight of stairs?"

She nodded, and I wrapped my arm around her waist. "Just lean into me. I'll give you support. When we get to the bottom of the steps, wait while I check things at the car. If he comes down the stairs, start screaming and get to the car as fast as you can." She was swaying against and away from me. I had to get her to a safe location.

We tottered down the last flight of stairs. "Hold on to this railing, Laura. Wait here. I'll be right back to get you. Don't step onto the car deck until I come to get you or unless he comes after you. Okay?" I left without looking back because I was not willing to see fear etched on her face. There was part of me that was laughing at Dev Rosten pretending to be brave, and another part of me was, in reality, fearless. I didn't need the fearless me derailed by Laura's terror.

Crouching low enough to keep my head below car roofs, I inched my way toward my car. It was parked two rows over and about six cars back. I peeked through car and truck windows looking for anyone tampering with my Lexus. Nobody was near the car as far as I could tell. I wended my way back to Laura.

We shuffled to the car. Just as we got there, the loudspeaker proclaimed we were docking on Lopez Island. "All passengers with Lopez Island as their destination must return to their vehicles."

"Perfect timing," I said as we settled back into our seats. I shoved the bloody tire iron under the seat.

"Dev, would you recognize a bomb if you saw one?" Laura had her head on the seat back.

"Do I really want to know why you ask?"

"Well, don't people like him use explosives? You probably think I'm being melodramatic, but taking out this car would be simple for him." Beneath her fear, I detected exhaustion, pain, and resignation.

"I'll look, but I have no idea what to look for." I opened my door. She was right. I had to at least look. I crawled out of the car and got on my hands and knees on the gritty deck. My first thought was of all the men that had spit right where my hands were placed. Then I figured dried spit was the least of my worries.

My knees didn't like the unforgiving deck floor, but I took my time and inspected the underside of the car from several different angles. I looked into the tire wells. Several people groused over and around me trying to get to their own vehicles. I was glad they were there because their presence gave me a sense of security.

My unskilled eye didn't detect anything foreign. I opened the hood and looked at the alien territory known as a car engine. Every gizmo in there looked like a bomb. So I closed it and whispered a prayer to any entity that cared.

"We have to check your car, ma'am." A woman came from behind. I spun around and was face-to-face with a short, stocky ferry security official. She wasn't the same security guard I'd met here on Monday. Her hair was pulled into a tight bun that stuck through the opening of her ball cap. She had an official security badge and a firearm hanging off her belt.

"Why? What have I done?" I'm sure I looked like I'd done it, whatever "it" was.

"We have reason to believe someone is injured on this ship. You will need to consent to a search, or we will have to detain you." She was one of those women who probably guzzled a beer and swore like a trooper just before she threw her husband into a wall. I wasn't going to argue.

"Officer, my friend is recuperating from an accident. See the bandages? Does she have to move?"

The little Attila went to Laura's door and opened it. She bent, took note of Laura's cast and bruises, and clicked the door shut. I willed myself not to sweat or shiver.

"Have you seen anyone pass by with immediate injuries, maybe bleeding?" She was inspecting my face for any sign of deception.

"No! Uh…no. I was just checking my car. I've been having some trouble with it." I patted the car hood. "It seems okay, though."

The guard nodded and without a word, moved to the next car.

"They've found the blood in the bathroom, but they haven't found him," I told Laura when I got in.

She had zipped her coat over the slice on her neck to hide it from the security guard. "That means he's still after us. Shouldn't we just tell her?" she said.

I reached across the seat and clutched her good hand for a few moments. "I wish we could. But the power of Stratton's people is widespread. We can't trust the police yet. But we'll make it out of this. I promise."

Her eyes were glazed with pain and fatigue. "Do you? What makes you so sure, psychic woman? Does your crystal vision make room for the kind of people who annihilate innocent people just to kill the one person they want dead?"

I had nothing to say to that, so I sat back and waited for the signal to start my engine and vacate the ferry. Soon I saw the traffic officer in his orange jacket wave us out of the ferry. Both Laura and I were looking in several directions to catch sight of the attacker. We were just leaving the car deck when a jarring crunch rocked our car.

We flinched, fearing an explosion. A hand splatted on the windshield and bloody fingers splayed. A crimson face, upside down, lurched into my line of sight. It was him. The gash from my tire iron had torn open his forehead. Blood oozed from it and onto the windshield in rivulets.

He smiled a sickening upside-down demon's grin. His teeth were tainted with blood. His other hand appeared and pounded the windshield in front of Laura. Blood spattered on Laura's side of the windshield. He looked insane. The glass in front of Laura spidered. His hands and face disappeared. A squeaking of damp skin pulled across car metal filled our ears.

In my rearview mirror, I saw the rugged security lady had pulled him off our car. He was rolling on the ferry deck, and she had her gun aimed at him.

Ferry personnel were signaling for us to stop. Instead, I pressed the windshield spray mist and turned on the wipers. The diluted blood was pushed away, leaving our view cleared of the vile red. Lots of it lingered where the wipers couldn't reach. I punched the gas, cut off a pickup just about to take the exit ramp, and tore my car out of there. I made a commitment to myself to buy that security toughie a drink someday.

"I know his name. I know who he is," Laura said while gingerly unzipping her jacket away from her neck.

"Why didn't you say so before? Who is he?" I had to keep my eyes on the road, which was a good thing because I was annoyed that Laura had held back information.

"Look, I've been injured…a head injury. They've put me on scads of drugs, and I'm running for my life. Excuse me if my lucidity is compromised."

"Sorry, sorry. I'm more than *fartootst* here. So help me with my confusion, because if we know his name, we can learn something about him." I felt guilty at sounding aggravated with Laura, but I was confused and scared.

Laura let out a tired breath. "His name is Tom Dwight. Last I knew about him, he worked for Jerry Greenfield."

"Why am I not shocked? How do you know this Dwight guy worked for Greenfield?" We were taking the road south that bisected most of the island, passing through the fields and woods that blanketed the terrain. It was raining again, enough that I turned my wipers to intermittent. Tom Dwight's blood left the windshield in pink, watery rivulets.

"Years ago, when Elizabeth and I broke up, I followed her romance with Greenfield in the newspapers. Dwight was occasionally with Greenfield in press photographs. They would refer to him as Greenfield's bodyguard. He was scary even back then, although in recent years I've seen no sign of him in the Greenfield press coverage." She was cradling her wrist again.

"Do you need more medication? We'll be at my place soon."

"Believe it or not, the pain is better. Maybe it's because

of the adrenaline. Right now, I just want to check my neck and see how bad it is."

"There's a mirror on your sun visor. Check it out. I think your neck got very lucky today." I was keeping my eyes open for anyone following us. No sign of any cars.

"Lucky? Are you going to wish me mazel tov?" She was dabbing at the cut with a tissue.

"Very funny. Listen, that guy knows people who will get him out of whatever little scrape he's into with the ferry security. He's delayed, but he'll be back and probably with a few friends. Do you know anything else about him?"

"I think one article said that he was a former soldier of fortune and he found God. He joined up with Jerry Greenfield as a bodyguard, I guess. Looks like he's gone back to his old profession."

"I doubt he ever left it. 'Found God' my ass." I pulled the car onto a dirt turn-around, parked but left the engine running. "Keep an eye out for anything. I have to do some communicating." First I texted Fitch asking for an update. Then I called my island security company, letting them know I'd be around for a few days. I also asked them to send their patrol car down the road to Tranquility several times a day. They quoted the extra fee, and I agreed. Lots of well-heeled people had homes on Lopez. Security was expensive but worth it given the isolation of some homes and the expensive belongings within them.

Before I could pull back onto the road, my phone buzzed signaling a text message from Fitch. "Situ wrs than thot. Whr r u? need 2 tlk." The third grade teacher still residing within me winced at the text spelling. I worried that people would carry those spelling habits into their formal writing.

I sent a return message, correctly spelled but with challenged punctuation, that I would call her in a few hours. I also texted two more words: "tom dwight." That was all Fitch would need.

We continued down Center Road past Lopez School and eventually took the turns that led us to Hunter Bay Road. When we reached the long driveway that led to my home, I pressed my key fob to open the security gate, then drove the car through and closed the gate with the fob.

The night Stratton had visited me, my world was different. That gate had been left open, a result of my naïve belief that island life was safe. I was never going to make that mistake again. I looked at Laura. Her profile exuded determination even though the circles under her eyes denoted fatigue. Maybe the event that called Laura into my life couldn't be designated a mistake.

We made our slow way down the graveled road to Tranquility. When I was within one thousand feet, I pressed another button on my fob and deactivated the house's security system. After passing through a few hundred feet of wooded area, we entered into the wild grass hillocks that comprised the yard of Tranquility.

"Oh, wow," Laura said when she caught sight of the contemporary architectural beauty of the house. "That's an awe-inspiring house, Dev. I was expecting some little rustic cabin with an outdoor toilet and kerosene lamps. This is anything but rustic."

"It took lots of planning, phone calls, schlepping, and a few tears, but I got it built. And everything is as green and sustainable as one can make it on an island. Plus, it has a world-class security system. We will be safe here until we can decide what our next move will be." The garage door purred open and we parked the Lexus with its cracked windshield and a few dabs of blood near the edge of the glass. "I'll call someone to come out and fix the windshield. We'll have to wash off Dwight's blood first. Nasty." I fought a nauseating revulsion.

"You really think he'll still come after us?"

"Probably. With reinforcements. Listen, when we get into the house and activate the security system, I'll make us something to eat. I have some food in the freezer and possibly a few potatoes. I'll need to make some calls too. And you'll need to get some rest. When we're fed and rested, we'll have a strategy session. Think you'll be up to it?"

Laura looked at me with a small glower. "We've gotten this far. But remember that my jury is still out on whether I can trust you or not." She crawled out of the car and slammed the door.

Something about her anger and resolve fueled in me an intense craving for her. I had always assumed it was impossible for me to feel craving toward anyone. I was having misgivings about being alone with Laura Bishop in my home. Somehow, I had to reconcile my assignment from Elizabeth Stratton with my feelings for Laura Bishop.

One Jewish saying kept grinding through my mind. "A half-truth is a whole lie." I had to tell Laura everything. But how?

CHAPTER TWELVE

We finally ensconced ourselves in Tranquility with the security system activated. I told Laura to make herself comfortable in the living room while I got dinner prepared. I left her to wander around checking out my art collection.

There were some flank steaks in the freezer that I quick-thawed in the microwave. After they were browned in a pan, I covered them with a can of diced tomatoes, browned onions, garlic, and water. I left the steaks to cook for a while. I threw a couple potatoes in the toaster oven to roast. I opened a bottle of cabernet and dumped a cup of it into the simmering steak dish. I poured two fragrant glasses of the wine and lamented to myself that it hadn't had time to breathe.

"Oh, well," I said. I carried the two glasses into the living room and set them on the same coffee table that held Elizabeth Stratton's check in the drawer. Laura was lying on the couch, her shoes off and a decorative pillow under her head.

"Antonin Prevot," she said.

"Excuse me?"

"Antonin Prevot. You have ten pieces by one of the most collectable artists of our generation. Granted, they're not like his usual work, but they're spectacular. They appear to have been made specifically for you. They're tarot themes, aren't they?"

I glanced at the mixed media pieces that graced the room's walls. I sat on the end of the couch near her feet. She scootched toward me a little and rested her feet on my lap.

"I'd buy you another Prevot if you'd just massage my feet now. I'll sign an I.O.U."

"No need to go into debt. If this helps you feel better, then it's my pleasure." I started working the pad of her foot through her sock.

"Who are you, Dev? How can you afford art like that?" Her eyes were closed, but her brows were pinched in concentration.

"I told you I'm one of a kind. I help a lot of people. They pay me a lot of money if they can afford it. If not, then we work out a trade."

"And Prevot traded his art for your services."

"Pretty much. But that's all I can tell you, and even that is confidential, Counselor. Can you maintain your lawyerly discretion?"

"What paintings?" She was smiling. I had rarely seen her do that. It felt good.

For a while, we stayed silent while I worked her feet. A couple of times she groaned when I hit a particularly satisfying spot. I glanced at her face and saw her looking at me, her chest visibly moving up and down with each breath. As if remembering where she was, she lurched upright and swung her feet off my lap and onto the floor.

"Whoa, uh, thanks for that." She shook her head and reached for her wine. "I only want a few sips, given all the pain meds in my body."

"Oh darn, I completely forgot about that. Sorry." I was

embarrassed by my lack of thoughtfulness. "Let me get you some juice, or tea. Soda? How about water?"

We both stood at the same time. She turned and headed to the kitchen. "No worries. I'll help myself." She vanished from the room in double time. I remained by the couch feeling dopey.

"Whoa!" I heard her yell from the kitchen. I rushed in to see what had impressed her. "You're a cook?" She gazed at my well-used and amply supplied kitchen.

"Yeah, I guess I am. Sometimes. I mean, I love doing it, but I'm often too lazy to go through the paces." I stepped close behind her and surveyed the kitchen too. "Besides my library, this is the room where I spend the most time." She leaned back into me as if it were as natural as relaxing into a chair. It was a satisfying and terrifying sensation. I didn't know what to do with my shaking hands, so I rested them on her waist.

"Why do I feel so comfortable with you, Dev? When you first came to the hospital room last night, you felt so, I don't know, so right. You're almost like a pleasant déjà vu. Like I've known you before. Is it just me?"

She had her head against my cheek. My mouth was a few inches from her ear. "No, it's not just you. I'm compelled to be here. With you. The reasons are complicated, but there's no other place for me to be but right here." I let my arms encircle her, and I held her close for a few luscious quiet minutes.

Beep, beep, beep. The cooking timer interrupted the moment of magic.

"Is the food ready?" She pushed away from me. She walked to the stove, grabbed a hot pad, and lifted the lid on the pan.

My body felt chilled where hers had just touched it. Like a comforting blanket torn off me in the middle of a freezing night. "Let's see if there are any veggies in the freezer. I'll heat them up, and by the time they're ready, the steak will be done. Oh, gosh, I hope you eat meat."

"I eat meat. Couldn't be a combative bitch attorney without chomping on flesh once in a while." She wasn't looking at me. She was embarrassed by having leaned into me.

"Have a seat. I'll serve the meal in a few minutes." I dug around the freezer. "Peas okay with your meat and potatoes?" I swung around to find her looking at my backside. She was definitely feeling better.

She looked away and nodded. "I'm actually hungry. I haven't had a real meal in two days, or a decent night's sleep."

"We'll fix all that shortly," I said.

"Hmm." Her reply said more than any words could have.

Laura's splint inhibited her use of a knife, so I had the task of cutting her meat into bite-sized bits.

"Here, let me give you the first bite," I said and raised a bite of meat to her lips. She wrapped her lips around the food and took it from the fork while never removing her gaze from my eyes. While she chewed, she closed her eyes and concentrated.

She swallowed. "That is astounding. So tender, succulent, and the flavor is perfect. What is it?"

"One of my mom's frugal dishes, flank steak supreme. Sounds a little low rent, but it fulfills all kinds of comfort food needs, doesn't it? And wait until you taste the potato with it. It's a *mechaieh*."

"A what?" She was proceeding to tuck into the rest of her food.

"*Mechaieh*. Rhymes with *messiah*. It means a great joy or pleasure. All my mom's dishes are *mechaiehs*."

Laura flashed a glance at me. "I'm beginning to think my being here with you is my *mechaieh*." We both offered shy smiles over that comment.

I drenched her baked potato in sour cream and butter according to her directions. Then I fixed my plate, grabbed a small canister, and shook yellow flakes over my food. Laura watched, looking appalled as more flakes covered my food like snow coating a meadow.

"What in the world are you doing to your delectable plate of food?" she said.

"Brewer's yeast. It's healthy for my system. Among other benefits, I get selenium and chromium, plus a host of B vitamins. And, to tell the truth, I've become addicted to the taste. It's like how salt is for some people. They have to have it on everything. I'm that way about brewer's yeast." I gave an extra shake of the yellow flakes to prove my point.

She eyed my now yellow food. "Well, good for you. Keep it away from my plate."

We ate in companionable silence until I noticed she was struggling to cut the hardened skin on her potato. "I need to have some of this," she said. "It's my favorite part."

"Here, I'll help." I reached over and used her fork and knife to cut the skin. Again, I put a bite into her mouth. This time a dab of sour cream remained on her lip. I didn't think, hesitate, or wring my hands. I just leaned in and licked that tiny bit of sour cream from her lip. "I can be your napkin too," I whispered.

Laura sighed as if something perfect had happened. Then she came to her senses, I supposed. "What are we doing?" she asked while pulling her head back. "Is this even smart? Someone is trying to kill me, and I'm here playing kissy licky face. I should be calling the police."

That alarmed me. "No, not the police. We can't trust them, not in this situation. First, we eat and rest. Then we make a plan."

"What plan? And as for resting, even though I have a battered body, the last thing on my mind is rest, especially with you around. What is this between us, anyway?"

"I'm not really sure I can explain it. I just know that it's almost irresistible for me. It's nothing I've experienced before. Do you feel it too?" I touched Laura's face, gently stroking the skin around the bandage covering the cut Tom Dwight had monstrously delivered.

Laura leaned into my hand. "Yes, but the last time I felt this kind of attraction, I was young, and I was badly burned by Elizabeth. I haven't felt truly attracted to anyone since. So this isn't normal for me. And now my face has been carved up by an animal." Welling tears made her eyes change to a deeper brown than I'd seen before.

"Oh, sweetheart, your lovely face will heal. You're only going to get more beautiful than you already are. Here, let me show you what I see." I held Laura's chin, thumbed away the tears, and looked into her eyes. We were lost in the electric moment. I think she needed to gain some authority in the situation. She stood so that she was looking down at me.

Laura ran her hand behind my neck and entangled it in my hair. She gripped my curls and pulled my head back. "Let's see what this is about." She bent and captured my mouth with hers. This kiss was not tentative. It was strong, sure. I felt like she was staking claim on me.

All my senses became attuned to the kiss. The fragrance of Laura's skin. The wild feel of her fingers knotting my hair. My lips were open and ready when her tongue briefly explored my mouth. I gasped and moaned when she broke the kiss.

"I assume you have a bedroom in this castle," Laura said into my ear.

"Are you sure about this?" I knew I was sure, but Laura was injured and in danger.

"If I don't survive this fiasco, I'll be really pissed off that I didn't make love one last time before leaving the world. So, yes, Dev, I'm sure."

I stood without a word, took Laura's hand, and led her up the short flight of stairs that led to the master bedroom. When we reached my expansive, windowed bedroom, Laura took a few seconds to note the king-sized bed with books piled haphazardly on both bedside tables.

"When the weather is clear, this view is better than downstairs. Right now, I'm glad we're fogged in because I want no distractions," I said.

"No distractions," she said as she turned to me.

Laura trembled as I pushed my hands under her shirt and smoothed her skin. We both knew, in her injured state, that most of the effort would be mine. But it wasn't an effort. It would be an unmitigated pleasure.

I worked her hoodie carefully over her breasts, trying not to jar her wrist. My center of need was throbbing between my legs. Abundant soaking below signaled my body was slipping out of control. Whatever I did to her, I would revel in it. I hoped she felt the same.

As if reading my mind, she gasped and said, "I want everything you can give me. All the moans. All the heat. All the wet. I want all of it." Her voice had a swooning quality.

I licked between Laura's breasts. "You have no bra. Perfect."

"I…I couldn't…get one on…one-handed."

"Then there is one tiny blessing from your fracture. And

I'll be sure to capitalize on it." I covered Laura's breast with my entire mouth and gently sucked, gauging the responsiveness of her breasts.

Laura groaned and pulled my head tighter to her breast. Good start, I thought.

"Let me take your shirt all the way off," I said.

"Take anything…anything you want. I don't want to stop. I can't." When she said that, I blessed the aphrodisiac effect of danger. Maybe Fitch was on to something with the torture and whip thing.

Taking care not to jar Laura's injuries, I worked her hoodie completely off and threw it aside. I had to stand there and look at her. "You're so stunning. I don't want to take my mouth off you, never mind my eyes."

"Then don't. I need the bed. Now." She was breathing as if fevered.

"Can you do this? Will I hurt you?" I returned my mouth to her taut nipple, not really caring what she answered.

Her voice caught at every breath. "Oh…parts of me will hurt worse if you don't take care of me now. Please."

"Here, sit on the bed." I sat Laura on the end of the huge bed and knelt in front of her. "If you need to stop, tell me. Okay?"

"That won't happen. I've never wanted anything so much in my life as being here right now." Laura looked into my eyes. We were at sea with no possibility for rescue. And it was okay. "Take me whenever, however you like," she said.

"I'd like you a million different ways. Lie down." I pulled off my shirt and was gratified at her nod of approval. Then I removed my pants and underpants at the same time.

Laura pushed herself completely onto the bed and rested her head on the pillow. I straddled her. "Lift and I'll remove your pants." I worked the sweats over her hips and gasped when I caught sight of Laura's lacy silk briefs. "These defy imagination."

"That's the point," Laura said. Her voice was raspy with desire.

She twitched when she felt my hands on her thighs. I spread her legs and took in the sight of her wetness and her heady aroma. Judging from the pulsing between my own legs, I knew I was as aroused as her.

I couldn't prolong the moment. My need to touch Laura Bishop had reached emergency status. I placed my fingers into her wet center and moved them up and down in her slick folds, landing on her clit for a few strokes. Without giving her a warning, I entered her with two fingers. Another solid hot push in, then out, in again. Over and over.

The blood rushing in my ears coupled with the extreme arousal between my legs almost caused me to miss the sound of Laura's labored breath. Her pelvis rose to meet each of my pushes.

I looked at her ecstatic face and noticed the cut on her neck. It kept her from looking down at me. Everything I did at that end of her body would be a surprise. I bent and circled her clit with my tongue. She cried out in grateful pleasure. I was aware of the tremors pulsating from her center as I alternately sucked and licked. My fingers thrust again and again into Laura's core.

She was gripping the bedspread with her good hand. Her body quaked, having lost its compass. Within a few minutes, her gathering release found purchase and tossed her into oblivion, over and over. Laura screamed. She was heedless of how she sounded. And when it was over, tears trickled from the corners of her eyes.

When I removed my fingers from inside, Laura gasped and whimpered, wanting to stay connected a little longer.

"Don't worry. I can go back there soon," I said as I blanketed Laura with my body. I covered her face with kisses ending with a deep, moist kiss on her mouth. The fragrance of her juices sent another swell of frenzy through both of us.

I pressed my swollen sex on her thigh and glided over her. I was so wet. Her leg was slick in seconds. Laura's broken wrist rested on the bed, but her good hand searched between our drenched bodies looking to possess me. Once she touched my engorged clit, it took only a few strokes. I tumbled into my own abyss of pleasure, moaning from deep within.

We lay silent, shuddering together for several minutes before Laura could speak.

"How…what happened? I've never been so wild, so out of control. Who are you, Dev?" More tears gathered, and Laura fought sobbing.

"Shh. Please don't. I won't go anywhere. We'll get through everything. Together. This was meant to be. We are *bashert.*" I nuzzled my head on Laura's shoulder.

"What does that mean?" Before I could explain, exhaustion overwhelmed her. The stress, pain medication, and rocking orgasm took their inevitable toll. "Oh, Dev, I'm so so tired. I think I need to sleep now."

"Of course. You should sleep. I'll hold you until you drift off. Then I'll make some calls downstairs. Okay?"

Laura couldn't muster a reply. We worked ourselves under the covers. I adjusted myself to Laura's side and pulled her close. After that, she was lost to sleep. I didn't get to explain that *bashert* meant *destiny*.

❖

I detested tearing myself away from Laura after our lovemaking. The silken texture of her hair in my fingers, her gentle sleep breath, and the intoxicating smell of sex fought to override the call of my responsibilities. But I had to talk to Fitch. When Laura was completely asleep, I extricated myself from her exquisite body. I found my robe and went down to my study. I'd left my cell phone in the bedroom, so I used my landline to make the call.

Fitch answered her phone after one ring.

"Damn, Rosten, where have you been? I've got information that isn't meant to ferment in a barrel until it's ready to drink."

"Sorry, I was, uh, distracted."

"I'll bet. I've traced Laura Bishop's spending habits to every high-end lingerie outfit on the Internet."

"You didn't." Fitch remained silent. "Okay, you did."

"From the smoky sound of your voice, you are the beneficiary of Bishop's wanton spending. Was she wearing any vinyl?"

"Don't start, Fitch. She's my fantasy, not yours." I updated Fitch on the Tom Dwight incident on the ferry. Then I asked what she had learned in her research.

I heard the clicking of a keyboard and pictured Fitch in her technology room that looked like the lair of a mad scientist. All it lacked were bubbling beakers connected by tubes. Then I remembered that Fitch really was a mad scientist.

"Who do you want me to start with? The Stratton cabal is pretty disturbing. I've got little on Stratton, of course, but there's a bit on Jerry Greenfield and Tom Dwight."

"What about Laura? Did you find anything else about her besides her spending habits?" I was annoyed with Fitch for prying into Laura's life, but I had asked her to do it.

"I think Bishop is pretty clean. She just slept with the wrong person. That was the story of my life until I took full control, if you catch my drift."

"I do and let's move on. Tell me about Tom Dwight."

"He is one scary dude. Grew up in Bumfuck, Texas, and managed to get in all kinds of juvie trouble. His parents dumped him on his uncle, Allen Dwight, who raised him in a white supremacist environment. The kid was burning crosses before we learned to shave our legs. Even Texas authorities were appalled and took little Tommy away from his uncle by age fifteen. Foster homes until eighteen, then Dwight disappears from public record for a while.

"It took a bit of digging on my part, but he finally resurfaced as a mercenary soldier. He did dirty work for a few nasty governments in Central and South America. Then he landed a job as a squad leader for Mohawk Security. That was about fifteen years ago. During that time he started writing religious tracts for a fundamental Christian outfit sponsored by Jerry Greenfield. Apparently, Tom Dwight found God, and Jerry Greenfield found Dwight. From then until now, he's been Greenfield's lackey and probably hatchet man. He's dangerous, Dev. He thinks Jesus is on his side because Greenfield is on his side."

"Huh. It just goes to show 'You can educate a fool but you can't make him think.'"

"Isn't that the truth? Is that one of your Talmud sayings?"

"Why should I think of something original when I've got Talmud to quote? Anything more about Elizabeth Stratton?"

"Stratton? No. I can't find a human interest word on her, except what's in an approved bio. Her life remains an outline on a clean white slate."

"Tell me about Greenfield."

"It's kind of the same story as Stratton: bland. Greenfield grew up in San Diego. Played soccer in high school. Decent grades got him into Pepperdine. He did well enough. Joined a fraternity and a few academic clubs. He earned a bachelor's in religious something or other, graduated, and went to a Baptist seminary in Oklahoma. That's where he apparently learned his phony Southern accent. But it's strange. In fact, it's strange about both characters, Stratton and Greenfield."

"At this point, nothing will surprise me about those two. Keep going," I said.

"Both the bios check out. School grades are perfectly submitted by all their teachers. Records show their sports scores. But there's no color."

"No color?"

"These are pretty controversial folks. You'd think there would be some people from their early years who remembered them and were itching to be interviewed. The press loves to dig into the flotsam of people's lives and print it for more prurient humans like me. There is nothing, and I mean nothing, of human interest about these two. Even a look on the Internet maps for their childhood homes comes up with vacant lots. The houses were demolished within the last twenty years.

"Everything I've learned is public record: school reports, newspapers, interviews that took place during their professional careers. But it's all bland, no red meat. What I'm trying to say is I think Stratton and Greenfield were groomed or...manufactured."

"What about love affairs? Didn't they have a boyfriend or girlfriend along the way? These are two attractive people. Surely there is someone willing to kiss and tell."

"Afraid not. The only romantic interlude either of them has had, besides with each other, is Stratton's affair with Laura Bishop. And there is no evidence to support even that, just Laura Bishop's word. And it looks to me like they're doing their best to erase that."

"Speaking of, are you going to Colorado?"

"At this very moment, I'm speaking to you from one of Denver's finest hotels. I plan to drive east in the morning, which is not all that long from now. I have a lead on some fundamentalist activity in the countryside that could be related to Greenfield. I won't bother you with details unless I find something worth sharing."

"You, Miss Leather Fetish, are going to one of the most conservative areas of the country. Try to be a little, uh, discreet. Okay?"

"Worry not, Devy. I'm going to dress like Little Miss Vanilla who is out for a sightseeing tour of ranches and cows."

"Stop with the Devy, will you?"

"Before I go to eastern Colorado, I have one other question. What about your business deal with Stratton? Having an affair with your and Stratton's target is not a good idea."

"Hey, I'm not having an affair with Laura Bishop." Getting a lecture from Fitch, of all people, annoyed me. Besides, I was no longer planning an affair with Laura. I wanted more than that.

"Excuse me, but you are not a sleep around kind of gal. Is this more than an affair?" Fitch said.

"Yes, probably. But I can satisfy Stratton. I'll keep Bishop here at Tranquility until things blow over."

"And you'll call the press when? Stratton needs taking down, Dev. I don't care about your business ethics."

"Ethics be damned. I agree. Now I need to go and carry on this misbegotten mission."

Disturbed, I said good-bye to Fitch and remained at my desk pondering what I had just learned.

Fitch's conjecture about Stratton and Greenfield jarred me. "Manufactured" was the same word I used to describe the

Theater and its characters. Could Stratton and Greenfield be some sort of product of the Malignity?

"Holy hell. 'As above, so below,'" I said aloud. The Magician's traditional symbolism. One arm pointing up, the other pointing down. What occurs in the heavens is mirrored on earth. I looked at my fingernails. At least they were intact on my customary plane of existence, and so were Stratton's and Greenfield's.

I barely completed the thought when I was thrown to the floor. My body was squeezed and elongated like it was being blown through a straw. The wracking sensation ended, and I looked up at the face of the High Priestess. She was baring her teeth. At least that's what I think she was doing until I understood she was smiling. Her teeth looked like they had been carved out of soap, a facsimile of teeth. She would always revolt me, no matter what her intentions were.

"I thought you'd improved my transition process," I croaked.

"When it suits us. But sometimes meddlers need to be reminded who controls them." That spectral grimace of hers was lifeless. The teeth were dust dry. That's what made me shiver. "You don't like my visage, meddler? It's not human enough for you? I am not human, thankfully, so I don't aspire to look exactly like one."

"Who are you, really?"

"Using your words, let us say I'm another client. You have a task that needs completion. You are on the path of failure, I'm afraid. You have not been careful." Her thin eyebrows jerked woodenly together in a rehearsed gesture of disapproval. "Was it not clear when you were conscripted?"

"You haven't given me word one about what you expect of me." I stood and faced her. This time I wouldn't cower.

"Then go," she said. "Go to your Theater and learn what needs to be done. It may already be too late to save your Laura Bishop. The Malignity is marching, marching fast." Again, without moving, she smashed my body into the pillar behind her throne. I felt my forehead clonk against the marble.

There was no sensation of the transition to Pento's Theater. Instead, I heard him say, "Are you bleeding, damsel?"

I was lying on my back with my hands covering my agonizing forehead. Venomous darts of pain ripped across my scalp. My throat emitted a pathetic sound between a moan and a scream. My hands felt sticky. I pulled them away to find my tapered, nail-less fingers covered with blood. At least the blood was the right color, but on closer inspection, there was a melting red gelatin quality to it. I rolled on my side and spewed partially digested flank steak into Pento's faux dirt. The vomit had a rubbery bounce to it that made me even more revolted, and I finished with dry heaves.

Depleted finally, I rocked myself several times to collect my damaged self so that I could, just barely, rise to my knees. I worked the gloppy blood between the tips of my fingers. "Can you stop this…this blood? It's all wrong, Pento."

I looked up at Pento and saw him twist his head so far around, he was looking back over his shoulder blades. It was horrific, like a demon possession, but it lasted only a second then his head snapped forward again. My bleeding stopped, literally dried up, leaving a tacky residue.

"My apologies, damsel. Most humans do not like to see me work. For some reason, the twisting of my head annoys them. However, I cannot help it. It is what happens when I create within the Theater." He reached his gloved hand to me, which I grasped and felt him effortlessly pull me to my feet. "Please tell me. A few times when you have come to the

Theater you acted as if you had been struck in the head. Why is that? I cannot seem to make the transition pleasant for you. It has never been like that."

"Never? Your 'lady' never slams people against marble surfaces before she ships them off to you? Maybe you figure that abuse will make us more docile, more amenable to your wishes. Well, guess what, Pento, that doesn't work. At least, it doesn't work with me." I was squeezing my appallingly deformed fingers into the palms of my hands.

"Abuse? Whatever do you mean? The Lady gives me strict directions never to abuse anyone in the meddler line."

"What do you think the Lady does when I make my little appearances before her throne? She sure isn't serving me tea and crumpets." I was stepping closer to him in my anger. He backed away.

"Tea and crumpets? Appearances?"

"Quit parroting me. Tell me exactly what's going on here. And what is a 'line' anyway?"

"A line is you, damsel. You are a line, the bloodline. Why do you not know that?"

"Pento, just who is 'the Lady' that you are talking about? We need some definitions of terms so that we are clear with each other." He appeared as bewildered as I.

"The goddess Isis, the High Priestess, Persephone. The keeper of wisdom. She can be cold, but not brutal. Unless she is worried." He hesitated. "Oh dear, she is worried."

"Well, she doesn't seem to get that I break. She keeps tossing me around like a discarded rag doll."

"Then things are worse than I knew. She must be troubled. She wants you to resolve the situation with the Malignity without delay."

"You need to tell her to back off, Pento. I will try to do as

I've been directed, but I can't if I'm wounded or my skull is cracked. Are you sure she's on our side?"

"Of that we can be certain. Despite her cruelty to you, she does not align herself with He-Who-Comes-Before. They are competitors. She does not usually get so demanding." Pento was shaking his head in a jerky rendition of bewilderment.

"The Magician, the number one of tarot major arcane, or whatever else he could be called. He is Jerry Greenfield, and Jerry is the Malignity. Is that right?"

"He is but a creature of the Malignity. There are many. The Malignity hates free choice, so it terrorizes humans. It seeks to manipulate humans through their ignorance, fear, and naïveté. It has human puppets it cultivates. For your understanding, the Magician is an aspect of the Malignity. Greenfield is just a puppet." Pento's face tried to do indignation.

"And the Malignity's puppets carve the letter *I* on people's faces," I said when I realized the *I* on Laura's face meant the number one. The number of the Magician in tarot.

"That may be, damsel. I know its puppets are recruited when they are young. They always have great hunger for power because they are hollow inside. Mostly, they come to a terrible end, but sometimes they become vicious rulers. They leave no place for those who question their tactics. Your very people suffered from one of those only decades ago, I think."

"Well, actually, my people have suffered from many of them. But the worst for Jews was Hitler. Some of our other oppressors were popes, imams, wild-eyed screamers of righteousness. Wait. You said I'm a bloodline."

"As are all the humans. They come from bloodlines, each specially gifted. At different times in human history, certain bloodlines are called upon to either disrupt or restore. You come from the meddler bloodline. In your system of tarot cards, damsel, you are called the Fool. Your line is often useful to us."

"Because I can appear and change the course of events without warning. My bloodline shows up anywhere and nowhere, like the Fool in tarot. But I'm guessing we and other bloodlines don't always follow your script. Do they, Pento? The plans of your kind are often foiled. Am I correct?"

"You are correct. It is the unpredictability of human free choice. We set the stage, but humans write the script. It is the way your world has been designed, to help you humans evolve."

"Evolve into what? What is the destination for human evolution?"

Here Pento became inert, like a figure in a wax museum— lifelike but eerily unreal. Had my question pushed too far? Did his battery run out?

As I waited in the stillness, not even the fake birds flew, I thought about the Magician I had encountered there in the Theater. He had Jerry Greenfield's ridiculous pompadour hair. The Magician was the ultimate manipulator using both reality and illusions. He could be as malevolent as any card in the deck given the right situation, a creature of the Malignity. But he wasn't the wild card. I was the wild card.

I took a long look at my ghastly fingers. "I have work to do. I'm ready to leave now." It was as simple as that. I found myself sitting on the floor of my study, looking at my fingernails.

Exhaustion overpowered me. I crawled to the couch that stood against the wall. When I was comfortable with an afghan covering me, I fell asleep with the sweet anticipation of joining Laura later. I wanted to make love with her one more time before we returned to Seattle.

CHAPTER THIRTEEN

The phone on my desk jolted me to rummy consciousness. I checked the clock and saw I had slept several hours. Morning light shone through the cracks between the drawn curtains. I tripped to my desk and grabbed the phone receiver, forgetting it was a quaint model connected to the cradle by a cord. The cradle hurled and crashed off the desk after me as I slumped on the couch, receiver in hand.

"Jeez, Rosten, are you okay? What's happening there?"

"I'm okay. I'm okay. What's up?" I was rubbing my forehead, trying to wake up.

"You have to speed things up. It's gotten bad here in Colorado. Real bad." I detected a twinge of panic in Fitch's usually controlled voice.

"How? Did the denizens of eastern Colorado come after you with rakes and pitchforks?"

"Not me. They did something far worse. Someone bombed a women's clinic about seventy miles east of Denver. It was in the middle of nowhere. There were first responders rushing around me during my entire drive eastward. I just followed them."

"What does that have to do with Stratton or Greenfield? Wait, you said a women's clinic? Oh shit."

"Yeah, oh shit. An exclusive abortion clinic posing as a fat farm for the wealthy. Where the rising Hollywood starlets and preachers' mistresses can get rid of their mistakes with none the wiser. Someone found out about it and took it out. Six people killed. Only two survived, a doctor and a nurse."

"And you suspect Jerry Greenfield? C'mon, Fitch. He's too public and not that stupid, is he?"

"I've set up my laptop and other equipment in a little motel along Highway 36. I'm picking up chatter that isn't all that cryptic. Greenfield might not be stupid, but his lackeys are. They're blabbing all over the airwaves. His people were involved, all right. And it's more than an anti-abortion operation. They were looking not only to destroy an abortion clinic, but to destroy all the clinic's records." Here Fitch went quiet while I spent a few moments connecting dots.

"I see," I said. "Looks like my hunch was right. Can you get to that doctor and nurse?" Fitch made a derisive sound as if I'd asked her if she could tie her own shoes. "Find out what they know. Feel free to tell them everything about your trip to Colorado, why you're there, Laura's situation, everything. I'm thinking they have a story to tell you and are willing to go public when it's safe. Do what you can to ensure their safety, and I'm not talking about the police."

"I'm on it. I've got security connections here. The doctor and nurse have been rushed to a hospital in Denver. My guess is I'll find them there and will need to get them out before someone lays waste to them. As soon as I get their story and have their safety secure, I'm flying back to Seattle. I'll charter a plane if I have to."

"You're amazing, old girl."

"I'm not old and I'm not a girl. I'll call you when I get to town. Touché, by the way." She hung up.

I sat on the couch for several minutes weighing my choices. How many times in my life had I asked myself the perennial question: If I could go back in time, when Hitler was a baby, would I kill him? Would the heinous act of killing an infant save six million Jews and countless others? I've never been able to answer that question. But I could answer this one: Would stopping the Stratton/Greenfield machine save anyone? Yes, it could save Laura, at least, and possibly others who dared get in the way of Stratton's campaign.

It became obvious to me that Elizabeth Stratton, Jerry Greenfield, and Tom Dwight were agents, puppets, of the Malignity. They all could go to hell, and I would be happy to have a hand in it. To me, they had become less than cockroaches. They'd been refined, groomed, and buffed to bring power to forces that loved to torment human beings. And I supposed, grudgingly, that I too had been seasoned to be the Fool, the wild card, the coyote, the trickster who spoiled the meticulous plans of humans and gods. I was the agent of chaos, either by naïveté or by cunning. But it was my choice whose plans I spoiled.

In those moments, I made my choice. I was going to take down Elizabeth Stratton and her machine. If my career, such as it was, ended, my clients disappeared, so be it. I opted for love and, in some larger sense, I chose my fellow human beings.

Determined, I left my office to find Laura. As soon as I walked out the door, I went straight to the living room and grabbed Elizabeth Stratton's check from the table drawer. I ripped it into the smallest pieces possible and tossed them into the fireplace. Time to hold Laura again, I thought, and started for the stairs leading up to my bedroom.

I was distracted by something glinting on the floor of the front foyer. My keys. My keys with the security fob. They had been on the dresser in my bedroom. My bedroom where I'd last seen Laura. Panicked with foreboding, I took the stairs two at a time and raced to the bedroom. It was abandoned.

Laura's clothes were gone. Her purse was gone. She was gone. My cell phone had disappeared too. They had gotten to her. While I slept, dreaming on my cozy couch, Stratton's animals had taken Laura. And I didn't do anything to stop them.

"No!" I screamed. I dropped to my knees and pressed my hand over my mouth. What could I do? My mind was wild with fear and guilt. I couldn't land on a thought, much less a plan. All I could think was I had to find Laura. Or they would kill her. If they hadn't already.

The jangle of my landline beside the bed pulled me out of my morass of indecision. I scrambled to answer it.

"Hey, Ms. Rosten? This is Pete down here at Island Security."

"Pete? Oh, Pete."

"Yeah, uh, the guys have been patrolling your property all night, real close like. All's A-okay. Do you want us to keep it up today?"

"They saw nobody? Nothing? All night?"

"Nothing at all. Your place is tight as a drum, but you need to turn your alarm back on. We noticed here in the office that your system got deactivated. But we figured you were there, so it was no big deal."

Could I trust my own security company? I wasn't sure, so I asked them to continue patrolling until further notice, regardless of the expense. He didn't complain. I didn't mention Laura.

Where would they take Laura? If the security team didn't see anyone in the vicinity of the house, how did they get to her? Would the security company lie to me? I strode to the curtains and yanked the cord. Before me spread Hunter Bay lit by morning light. The rain had run itself out. I scanned the bay looking for any kind of a watercraft, but much of the water was hidden by mist.

I pushed my forehead against the glass to peer down at my dock. My dinghy was gone. I rushed to my closet and grabbed the binoculars. When I focused them on the dock, I discerned that the door of the shed was hanging open. Someone had taken Laura and my boat. Maybe my boat had already been gone when we had arrived yesterday, a victim of a random crime. Maybe not.

I pulled the binoculars away from my face to keep a sudden vertigo at bay. When the dizziness passed, I used the binocs again and saw it. Just the tip of the bow was peeking from behind the rock several hundred feet out and to the right of the dock. I was sure that was my boat.

"What the hell? Oh God." I strung the binoculars around my neck, ran to the closet again, and found my boat shoes. I worked them on trying to hurry but not lose my head. If Dwight or one of his boys was in the boat with Laura, I had to handle it somehow. But to tell the truth, I had no plan. I just needed to get Laura back. She was all that mattered. Not Stratton. Not the High Priestess. Not Pento. Just Laura, only Laura.

I tore to the basement and out the back door to the little patio underneath the back of the house. The small area was strewn with spilled garden tools. I usually kept them on a shelf attached to the house, but someone had rifled through them and tossed them to the ground. Why garden tools?

I took the ladder down to the dock with my back to the water, all the time worried I'd be spotted by whoever was in the dinghy. I thought of Laura being forced down the ladder at gunpoint and my heart twisted for her. She was injured, in a cast, and probably witlessly scared.

When I touched the rock at the bottom, my foot slid out from under me, causing me to hang up briefly on the railings. I looked down and found a bandage stuck to the bottom of my shoe. Laura's bandage, the one from her face.

The sight of that woeful bandage, sodden and smudged, awoke every cowardly cell that dwelled in my body. Who was I to think I could save anyone? I had bad knees. I should save myself and not worry about anyone else.

"But it's Laura," I said aloud. I recalled Laura, in my bed, vulnerable yet strong, crying out in her release. Her eyes said more to me than a thousand love poems. "Yeah, it's Laura."

My resolve galvanized, I ran to the end of the dock, almost tripping on an abandoned flashlight. Someone had taken her when it was still dark. I used the binocs to observe the dinghy. It looked empty, but I could tell the cover tarp had been thrown back. Then I detected an odd shape. Someone wearing Laura's hoodie was lying on the seat.

"Laura! Laura, over here!" I shouted and waved my arms, jumping around like a fool at a rock concert. "Laura, are you all right? Hey, honey, sit up. Can you sit up?"

I didn't ask myself why Laura was out there. I just knew she was in trouble. After all, who would one-handedly take a dinghy out into the bay and then nap on the uncomfortable seat in the rain? This had to be trouble.

I cupped my hands around my mouth and upped my volume. "Laura! Laaaura!"

No movement. The little dinghy was slipping into the mist and would be lost to sight soon. Something was horribly wrong. How could I get to her? I dashed to the shed, barely registering that the hasp had been pried off. Standing nobly in the corner was the red standup paddleboard I had bought in the spring and used twice: once to try it out and once to learn how much I hated it.

I dragged it outside and leaned it against the shed. Then I retrieved the paddle and rested it alongside the board. Taking two trips, I schlepped the board and its long paddle to the miniscule beach near the dock. I dreaded the next part. I had no time to put on a wet suit or the special water slippers I'd bought along with the board. That water was torturous, around fifty-five degrees. My boat shoes, yoga pants, and sweatshirt would have to do.

The odious paddleboard was unwieldy for me, so I stumbled a few times while getting it positioned to drag into the water, the freezing water. I was sweating and planning to walk into icy Puget Sound waters. For a few seconds, a neon caution sign flashed in my head, "Hypothermia, hypothermia!" but I flipped a mental off switch and remembered I was saving Laura.

"Don't think," I said to myself as I started into the water. The iciness surrounding my feet made me suppress a scream, then my ankles, knees, and thighs all were submerged into the sharp cold ocean water. I was now in deep enough to use the board, but I had to will my frozen limbs to lift me onto my knees on the board.

I wasn't about to attempt standing up on that thing. It was a maneuver I had yet to master and probably never would. Kneeling with my butt on my heels, I wielded the long paddle and made my way out to the dinghy where Laura lay motionless. The paddleboard rocked beneath me. Every few strokes I was nearly tossed off.

"Laura, can you hear me?" I called, still a hundred feet away. Her stillness scared me more than anything I'd ever suffered before. That fear awoke every particle of my heritage, and I began to pray through chattering teeth, "Baruch Atah Adonai Eloheinu Melech Ha-Olam…"

The big Adonai in the sky must have heard me because I saw Laura twitch. "Laura, sweetheart, get up. Look at me."

I was almost upon her when she sat up, made one narrow glare at me, and hurled a pair of garden clippers smack into my forehead. The force knocked me off the board and into the frigidity of Puget Sound waters.

Cutting cold froze my scream. I gasped and sputtered as I struggled to get a stiffened arm over the paddleboard. I worked my second arm over the board, but I was too frozen to lift myself back onto the board. I hadn't mastered that maneuver wearing a wet suit. It was impossible to do it this time.

Laura had a terror-stricken appearance mixed with wrath. My jaw shuddered so violently, I could barely speak. "W-w-why? L-Laura?"

"I believed in you. You…you unspeakable liar. And I trusted you." Laura's tears glittered silver in the dull light.

"W-what are you t-t-talking about? N-never mind. Help me. P-please." My hands couldn't grip that board much longer.

"Why should I? You're planning to set me up, give me over to Tom Dwight, to Elizabeth Stratton. I heard what you said on the phone, Dev. I heard you. So I escaped. Get away."

What had I said on the phone? I'd only talked to Fitch when I was in my office. My brain was addled. I could hardly remember the gist of the conversation. Something about a bombed abortion clinic, dead people, and my having more feelings for Laura than a tawdry fling.

"You heard it wr-wrong. G-get me out of this w-water. D-do you want m-me to die?" Laura's eyes widened with the thought that my death would be on her hands. "P-please, Laura.

Remember, I s-said we are *b-bashert*. Destiny. M-meant for each other."

She reached into the bottom of the boat and reluctantly lifted the oar over the side and held it out to me. "Okay, you can get in the boat, but that doesn't mean I trust you. I just don't want to kill anybody even though, right now, it would feel really good."

I grabbed the oar with one hand, forcing my numb and stiffened fingers to hold on. I brought the other hand to the flare of the boat. Laura had only one hand, so I knew the onus of the effort would be on me. It took several bruising attempts, but I finally pulled my frozen self into the boat and slumped in the hull. My head rested on the gunwale, and I silently vowed never to get on a paddleboard again.

"Y-you could've helped a little more," I said. I looked up at her to discover she was ready to defend herself with a garden tool. "Hey, that's my b-brand-new Japanese cuttlefish hoe." Its spindly fingers pointed at my face. I couldn't decide whether to laugh or get mad. I emitted a shuddering, jittery laugh. She sat on the rear seat with a determined grimace. "That explains the garden tool mess on the patio."

"This is not funny, Devorah Rosten. You're in cahoots with Elizabeth and Tom Dwight. I heard you on the phone talking about the 'mission.'"

"The mission?" I thought for a few moments and remembered what I had said to Fitch. "Oh, that. I admit, at first I—"

Something hit the boat next to my cheek. I rolled my head to the left and saw a splatted dent in the gunwale about five inches from my face. Laura looked at the dent and then up to the cliffs. I looked too and, through the mist, could make out Tom Dwight taking aim at us with a rifle.

"Paddle!" I shouted at Laura. She dropped the garden tool

and clumsily put her oar into the water and started paddling. But I realized I had to be the paddler since I actually had two working hands. Another bullet ripped across the top of my forearm, spurting some blood but not debilitating me. Fright muted the pain. I grabbed the oar, scooted onto the center seat, and started working the oar first left, then right. "We have to get into the mist where he can't see us."

I glanced back to find she had a wooden paddle and was mimicking my moves as well as she could one-handedly. I heard three more splat-thunks in the water. Dwight's bullets. But we were buried in the mist. He couldn't see us.

Laura quit paddling. "Why should I go anywhere with you?"

Thunk. Another bullet hit the boat.

"Quiet," I whispered. "He can hear us." The mist may have hidden us from Dwight's view, but it also carried sound to the top of the cliffs. My arm was bleeding but not in huge volumes. It was beginning to hurt, though, a lot.

Laura discarded her unwieldy paddle and again threatened me with the hand hoe. In a seething whisper, she ordered, "Get us out of here. Now!"

I wasn't too worried about the garden implement, but I agreed we needed to move. The mist was so thick that it would be easy to become lost. So I registered where the cliffs were, turned the boat in the opposite direction, and silently began to paddle. My forearm stung, sending shots of pain up to my bicep. The back of my neck tingled as I sensed the garden tool nearby and the hideous possibility of a bullet severing my spinal cord.

I paddled in silence for several minutes, hoping I wasn't going in a circle and heading back into Tom Dwight's shooting range. At one point, I felt sweat running down my nose and took a swipe at it with my soggy sleeve. I brought away blood.

I had a cut from the clippers Laura had pitched at me. The blood must have been temporarily stanched by the icy water, but now it flowed freely.

"You wouldn't happen to have something for my wounds, would you?" I turned around to show her my dramatic cut. She flinched, then pulled her fashionably roomy bag from behind her seat. She rummaged around in it and came up with a wadded bandana that had probably been in there for months.

"Here, I've barely used it," she said as she handed it to me.

"Barely was not what I was hoping for, but I'll take it." I rested the oar and stretched out the crusty bandana so it would be long enough to tie around my head. I would have to ignore my arm injury for now. It wasn't bleeding much. I knotted the disreputable bandana to my head to soak up the blood. "Will you let me explain, Laura?"

"Keep your mouth shut, Dev. You said he could hear us, remember?" she said through clenched teeth and scraped the claws of the gleaming garden tool in my direction.

"We're far enough away for me to speak softly. I'm sure of it."

"Where are you taking us? To Jerry Greenfield's church so we can enter into their kingdom of heaven?" For me, her anger magnified her beauty.

"Look, we are on the same side. Completely. I'm not sure where I'm taking us, except away from Dwight's gun. I think if I can get us across the bay, we can get some help. We need to get to town, to the press." I was speaking in a squeaky whisper.

"That's what I've wanted to do all along. Why the change of heart? Did Elizabeth give you different marching orders?" She was really hurt at the thought of my being in the Stratton camp.

"Listen to me. I'm going to tell you the whole story, the absolute truth. When I'm done, you decide whether to trust me or not."

"Okay, tell me. But remember, this thing can remove an eyeball." She waved the tool at me. "And keep paddling."

I paddled, ignoring the pain in my arm, and told her the whole story, about my trips to the Theater and the High Priestess, the Magician, and Pento. I explained to her about my role as a meddler against the Malignity. I told her how Elizabeth Stratton handed me $125,000 with the promise of more if I derailed Laura.

"And now you, Laura. You have to tell me all of it. I'm not the only one who was holding back information. Hushing up your relationship with Stratton isn't worth a quarter of a million dollars."

Laura finally lowered the garden tool. She stared into the water. "I went with her. She said she needed me. We weren't even together anymore. We'd been apart for a year. She was a senator." She was speaking more to the water than to me.

"Stratton?" Laura nodded. "Where did you go with her?"

"To Colorado. To the clinic. She was pregnant. She aborted Jerry Greenfield's child."

The puzzle was complete. Senator Elizabeth Stratton, supposedly God's own candidate, had a secret so explosive, it would end her presidential hopes and political apparatus. If her followers knew she'd had a clandestine abortion, they would reject her without looking back, without forgiveness. The fact that it was Jerry Greenfield's child, an heir to the throne of the righteous, would make the firestorm even worse. Greenfield would be implicated. No matter what the Malignity had planned for Stratton, her choices were out of its control.

"No wonder they want you dead," I said. "Laura, do you have proof that this abortion happened?"

She nodded. "It's in the last few pages of the scrapbook, the pages I didn't show you." She looked world-weary and defeated.

"Describe what's there. What evidence do you have?"

"There's a clinic confidentiality agreement, signed by me. I also pasted in a plastic hospital bracelet from the clinic. It has 'E. Wilford' on it. That's Elizabeth's mother's maiden name."

"That's hardly enough to make a case. What else is there, Laura?"

She sighed. "Before we left the clinic, Elizabeth was pretty out of it, shaken and in pain, I guess. Since I was there as her escort, the nurse gave me two bottles of pills for Elizabeth to take for pain or excessive bleeding. If you remember, eight years ago, Elizabeth was already famous as the senator for the religious right."

"Oh, I remember. I even saw her one day when I did a reading for a client. She came to the hotel where the client and I met. Even then, she and Greenfield were repulsive."

"Please understand. Elizabeth wasn't always like that. She was good to me, until she wasn't." Laura was now hugging herself, shivering as if she'd just emerged from the icy water.

"Tell me about the rest of the evidence, Laura. You said you were given some pills?"

"Yes, two bottles of pills, unlabeled except for the drug name. But they also gave me two prescriptions to fill, in case Elizabeth needed more while she recuperated in a Denver hotel. I put the prescriptions in my purse and, frankly, forgot about them. Being around Elizabeth in such a strained situation, well, I wasn't thinking too clearly."

"Did you have the prescriptions filled?"

She shook her head. "Elizabeth bounced back quickly. She took a few pills from the bottles but didn't even need all of them. She never mentioned the prescriptions. They stayed in my purse. When I finally got back to Seattle, it was a few days before I found them."

"And they were written for Elizabeth Wilford? Using her mother's maiden name again?"

"No. For whatever reason, maybe for the use we have for them now, the doctor made the prescriptions out on his prescription pad. The prescriptions had the clinic heading plus the doctor's name. More importantly, they were made out to Elizabeth Stratton. The doctor had written Elizabeth's real name." Laura drew her knees up to her face and rested her forehead on them.

"The bombed abortion clinic," I said.

Laura looked at me in alarm. "What do you mean?"

"Yesterday, in Colorado, an exclusive abortion clinic was bombed. Four people died. However, the doctor and one nurse survived."

"We have to get to them. They're in danger." Laura started scrabbling for a paddle.

I grabbed the paddle. "Wait. It's okay. I have one of my associates lining up security for them. She's more than competent. I'm sure the doctor and nurse are safe. Actually, they're probably safer than we are right now." I looked around, but the mist still hid our whereabouts.

"I should have exposed her earlier. It's my fault people are dead. My fault." Laura's despair was excruciating to watch, but I could understand her feelings. I also knew she was wrong.

"Laura, honey, listen to me. These are the type of people who will stop at nothing. They've already saturated our country with enough righteous lies and propaganda to polarize people who used to be friendly toward each other. They want power at any cost. Do you really think wasting a few innocent lives is beyond them? If it weren't the security guards at Smith Tower or the abortion clinic, it would be something or someone else. We have to stop them, or there'll be more killing while they accumulate and consolidate power. I think our only chance is to go public with your evidence."

"Why Elizabeth? Why couldn't I see what she was?"

"Oh, you knew her well, better than anybody. I have a theory. I think Stratton went wrong on them somehow. They groomed her, but they didn't factor in her attraction to women. The night Stratton hired me, she made me promise that you wouldn't be hurt. I believe, in her warped way, she still loves you. I also think Tom Dwight is operating beyond her and Greenfield's control. He's their wild card unleashed, just like I'm a wild card unleashed."

I stopped paddling and turned around to face her. "The one thing the Malignity can't battle or understand is love, the most indestructible power of all. Elizabeth was groomed for authority, but they forgot to immunize her against her love for women. It is her so-called weakness that will, in the end, bring her down. Had she not hired me to gently meddle with you, Tom Dwight would have destroyed your scrapbook and your life days ago." I waited for Laura to grasp what I was trying to say to her.

She looked steadily at me, measuring the validity of my words. "How did your meddling, or whatever you call it, save me?"

"They thought I was on their side. I was a meddler, conscripted by Stratton, to distract you. They had no idea I'd already been in contact with the High Priestess and Pento. A result of my wild card status, I guess. If anything, the Malignity thought I would march you right into Dwight's gnarly arms, even if Stratton wouldn't fully agree to that."

"I'm still not getting it, Dev."

"Every time the High Priestess tossed me from her throne room into the Theater, I would have an experience that included you. That's where I became enamored with you. That's why I got you out of that hospital room before Dwight got to you. I can't resist you. They didn't factor it in. The Malignity and its puppets do not understand love. They didn't think I'd try to save you or that I'd fall in love with you."

Before she could respond to my risky declaration, her attention was caught by something behind me. I turned just before the boat rammed into a pontoon. The pontoon was attached to a seaplane.

❖

All we had were the dubious contents of Laura's bag, which contained, besides essential womanly things, my cell phone that she stole from my bedroom, her forbidden credit card and checkbook, and the garden tool. However, the owner of the airplane managed a labyrinthine telephone exchange to assure himself that Laura's check would cover the outrageous sum of $2,000 for the thirty-five minute flight to Seattle. He also managed to produce a bandage for my arm.

"You ladies need to understand something here. It's foggy out there. It's Thursday, my day off, and I promised my better half I'd fly her to Anacortes to have lunch. So my flyin' you to Seattle takes a big bite out of my day. See? Besides, looks to me like you're in a hurry." His belly jiggled loosely over his cowboy belt, and his stained Seahawks ball cap was slightly askew. I hoped we wouldn't have to meet his "better half."

"We need to leave immediately. Can we do that, Mr., uh, Mr.?" Laura was handling the negotiations because she looked less disheveled after our adventure in the bay.

"Haney. Bill Haney. My plane's called Jenny, after my

daughter. She lives in Bellingham, teaches at the high school there, has two kids, both bright as—"

"Do you have to make any preparations, Mr. Haney? We really do need to leave." Laura wasn't going to let him ramble on. She was an attorney even in dire emergencies.

"Ah, call me Bill, honey. All the lovely ladies call me Bill. Hell, we're almost all prepped to fly anyway since I was supposed to fly to Anacortes. You pretty things just wait by the plane while I get my gear and give the wife a quick one." He snickered and walked into his house, from which billowed odors of fried bacon and burnt toast.

When he was out of hearing, Laura and I made our plan for when we landed on Lake Union in Seattle. It was simple. We would head to my bank via cab, retrieve the scrapbook and recorder, and then call press acquaintances Laura had at the *Seattle Herald* and Channel 10.

We should have viewed the flight in Bill Haney's seaplane as foreshadowing the folly of our plans. Haney decided we were on a joyride instead of a business trip, so he made it as nauseating as possible in a flying apparatus with huge pontoons swinging off the bottom. He looped, cut the engine, and plunged altitude enough times that Laura and I were grateful our stomachs were empty. Laura sported a green tinge in her cheeks. Haney was gleeful and unrepentant.

By the time we passed over the Ballard and Fremont neighborhoods and spied the rusted tangle of Gasworks Park, we would have paid Bill Haney another $2,000 just to let us out of his flying carnival ride. The spraying touchdown on Lake Union reminded me of a debauched Disney waterslide. Passengers on surrounding leisure boats glared at our inappropriate arrival. I never thought I'd be so thrilled to see the Space Needle rising above Seattle's uptown in all its 1960s splendor.

I probably swore in Yiddish during the flight because when we bid our relieved adieus to Haney, he said, "La Hi Em to you, pretty ladies. Happy Chanukah, or whatever it is you people say to each other." He was a putz, but he got us there alive.

CHAPTER FOURTEEN

Go ahead and use my cell phone since you saw fit to steal it from my bedroom. Maybe they won't be tracing it, but who can be sure at this point?" I said.

Laura called a cab, and like two tattered refugees, we hid behind a service van and waited for the taxi to arrive.

"The driver is going to think we're homeless wretches," said Laura.

"We kinda are. Do you have a brush? Look at my hair." I checked myself in the van's side mirror. I'd lost Laura's ugly bandana in Haney's plane.

"Not one that will pull through that tangle of yours, but I do have a hair band. That should make you look less feral, anyway." She dug clumsily through her bag.

"Here, let me help." I reached to hold the bag for Laura. But Laura snatched the bag away before I could touch it.

"Can I really trust you? How can I believe the bizarre things you've told me? Nobody has visions, and definitely, nobody visits tarot characters."

I was wounded by her doubt. "But I do. I really honestly do." I took the hair band from Laura and twisted back my matted locks. "Hey, even if you don't believe how I got here, just believe that I'm here to help you. I don't want Senator Stratton running this country any more than you do. And my life is on the line now too. I know more about Stratton than is safe. On top of all that, Laura, you mean everything to me."

Laura didn't argue with my reasoning. She looked pained. "Maybe I don't like the idea of separating from you, but that will change if you prove to be a liar." She fiddled with the new bandage she'd put on her face. "Do you really want to be seen with someone who has Frankenstein stitches on her face?"

"Yes. Absolutely. Besides, when they heal, you'll hardly be able to see them. By the way, that isn't the letter *I* carved in your face, you know." I inspected the wound. "It's the Roman numeral for the number one, the number of the Magician. He is a *macher* of the Malignity, one of the big cheeses."

"Why carve it on my face or the faces of the security guards in the Smith Tower?"

"I think that was Tom Dwight. He's their Knight of Swords. He's sadistic and slipping out of their control. Otherwise, he wouldn't be scratching the symbol for the Magician on his victims. It's too blatant. Dwight feels invincible, making him dangerous to both sides. The sooner he's stopped, the better." I glanced at the parking lot. "Here's our cab. Are you ready for this, honey?"

"Keep calling me 'honey' and I might follow you anywhere."

"You're kind of easy, you know that?"

"I'm wounded, hunted, and scared. But with you, it's not quite so bad." Laura thought for a moment. "Not that you're any great warrior or anything. You're just awfully adorable."

"If that's what it takes to keep you with me, I'll continue with adorable. It's in my skill set. Let's get in the cab now." I grabbed Laura's hand and helped her into the backseat of the yellow cab.

As the cab wound through Seattle's mazelike streets to get downtown, Laura could sense my tension mounting. I grumbled and twitched at each traffic delay. "In any sane city, the short distance from Lake Union to downtown would take a couple minutes. But not here. Not on Seattle's *meshugana* streets. Drives me nuts."

"Listen to you, Dev. Be patient. We'll be at the bank soon. After that, all Hades will break loose when we face the press. I'll call them as soon as we recover the scrapbook and recorder." Laura was pensive for a few minutes. "Wow, I'm going to need an attorney. I'm making some calls while we wait in this traffic."

"Can you keep me out of the publicity?" I was panicked at the thought of my work being exposed. Laura seemed to think I would bolt from the car, because she held my wrist.

Laura pondered my fears for a few minutes. "For now, I think this is probably just my story. There is no way the public will buy your side of things. So, okay, but you can't ditch me." Laura gave me a steely glare.

"I promise. I'm with you no matter what." I didn't tell her that I would even sacrifice my profession to be with her. It was one card I held in reserve.

Laura used my phone's Internet apps to find the number for an attorney. When she called, she sounded like she was sitting at her office desk instead of on the run from a murderous maniac. She retained the attorney within a few minutes.

"His name is Jack Ramirez. Fabulous attorney. Good thing he's a buddy of mine. He promised to meet with us at the bank. His office is a block away. You okay with that?"

I didn't answer. We had finally arrived at the bank in Pioneer Square, and I was scanning the sidewalk in front of the building. "Don't stop," I ordered the confused cabbie. "Drop us a couple blocks away." The cab lurched back into traffic.

Laura heard the shaking in my voice. We both looked back at the bank. Two young skinheads were watching the cab pull away. One of them was using a phone while he traced the cab's path.

"Shit, shit, shit." I looked around the streets for a place to go. "Pay him, Laura." Then to the cabbie I said, "Go around that corner, and we're jumping out of here. You keep going and don't stop until you're out of downtown. Okay?" The cabbie nodded and took forty dollars from Laura, twice the fee on the meter.

"That's the last of our cash," she said.

The cabbie pulled the car into an unloading zone, and Laura followed me out of the car. We hustled into an alleyway and peeked around the old brick building to the street. Far down the block, the two skinheads in army green were searching the street and inspecting all the pedestrians.

Laura grabbed my shoulder. "I'm having vertigo, Dev. I can't do this." There were beads of sweat on her forehead, and her hands were shaking. The rank urine smell of the alley probably heightened her light-headedness. It wasn't thrilling me either.

"You have to, honey. C'mon, this way." I guided Laura down the alley toward a group of a few dozen people gathered expectantly outside the ramshackle back door of a turn-of-the-century building. "Don't talk, Laura, just bury yourself in this group. Act like you belong." Easy for me to say since my heart felt like it was going to blow any minute.

"Belong to what?" Laura muttered. She looked a little less peaked.

"The Underground Tour. Pretend you're a tourist. Look interested." I spoke between clenched teeth. We were now at the edge of the group and working our way around to the far side, away from the end of the alley and the skinheads.

"I'm not going down there," Laura whispered. "Do you know what's down there? A basement with rats. I hate basements. And I really hate rats." She stiffened against my insistent push to her lower back.

"Good, someone other than me has a phobia." A few of the tour participants were frowning at us. "Now buck up. Please, Laura." I looked up at the tour guide, who had just finished his witty spiel, causing the crowd to chuckle as they dutifully filed into the deteriorated door the guide had opened. I gave Laura a more forceful push, and she gave way, heading into the door with the happy tour crowd. She gave me one simmering stare, then started down the dusty wooden steps into Underground Seattle.

Our senses were assailed by the odor of wet dirt, damp brick, and mildew. Laura shuddered. However, as she followed the group down the creaking stairs. I could tell her vertigo was diminishing because she went down the stairs without using the railing. She sensed me close behind her and reached back to grab my hand.

I leaned forward to speak into Laura's ear. "What do people get out of this place anyway? They paid for this?" We continued to follow the crowd along a wooden plank walkway. On one side dimly lit black-and-white photos of old Seattle during the late 1800s hung on the decaying brick wall. On the other side of the walkway was decrepit flooring, sometimes dirt, sometimes wood and cement.

"Keep moving, folks," the tour guide hollered. "Wait for the group when you get to the next room, the one with the red sofa."

I couldn't believe there was a red sofa somewhere in this squalor, but we kept moving. We saw old-time hand-painted signs pointing to various long-dead businesses. I recalled that this neighborhood of Seattle had once been one story lower than present-day buildings. Where we were walking underground had actually been outside at street level. Storefronts that had been covered over for a hundred years still had their floors, windows, and bits of decrepit equipment. There were paint-peeled doors leading to places this tour would never go because those areas were dangerous or still used as basements for current businesses. I had once heard that only a small portion of the Underground was viewed by tourists. I was disturbed at the thought of what lay behind those doors and boarded-up passageways.

Finally, our group reached the dusty red brocade sofa, a reminder that much of Underground Seattle had been used as brothels and opium dens. The tourists gathered around it, gawking as if it were a zoo animal.

"Of course, this is not a vintage sofa from the era," the guide said. "It was placed here to give you all the idea of what really went on in Underground Seattle when it was still a lively place." The group tittered and shook off being duped by the tour operators. They all started wandering around the space, as if spidery ceiling joists and defunct plumbing held deep interest. I just wanted to find another way out. Laura and I hovered, arm in arm, at the edge of the grungy room.

Somebody cleared his voice behind us. "Excuse me, ladies. I don't want to inconvenience you, but could you show me your tickets?" The tour guide looked down on us with smug disapproval. He knew we didn't belong to the group.

"I'm sorry," Laura said, "but aren't you supposed to sell us our tickets? We thought you sold them down here." Bless Laura for her quick thinking. Her strength and resilience became more amazing every hour. "We've been waiting for you to take our money."

The guide didn't even attempt to disguise his eye roll. "You're supposed to start the tour at Doc Maynard's, the business upstairs on Pioneer Square." I'm sure we looked like a couple of down-and-outs just trying to find somewhere to kill time.

"But we love your way of delivering the tour. Your speech was so clever and interesting. We just had to have you for our guide." Laura used her most wide-eyed innocent voice. She had no idea the bandage on her stitched face made her look less than trustworthy.

The guide glanced at her cheek and at her splinted wrist. "Well, I don't want you wandering around here alone. It's too dangerous. So stay with me now, and when we come out of this leg of the tour, you'll have to go buy tickets and pick up with the next guide." He trotted back to the rest of the group.

"Like I want to spend good money gazing at abandoned toilets," I said.

"I think it's kind of interesting. Maybe someday—" A crash startled all of us in the tour. It came from the direction of their initial entrance. Heavy boots clunked on the wooden walkway.

"Over here. Now." I grabbed Laura's upper arm and dragged her behind a huge piece of moldy plywood leaning against the wall farthest from the walkway. "Don't move," I whispered. We cowered behind the plywood, our backs against an unspeakable section of rotting wall.

"Excuse me, gentlemen, but we're having a tour here. Buy your tickets at Doc Maynard's, please." The impotent tour guide tried to assert himself. I would have snickered under normal circumstances.

"Shut the fuck up, asshole," said a voice I assumed came from one of the skinhead predators. "We're looking for the two fuckin' ladies who joined your fuckin' group. Where are they?" We heard heavy steps pass by us, heading toward the tour guide.

The whole tour group gasped as one. The guide squeaked. "I kicked them out. I kicked them out. They didn't pay. They're gone. See? Not here."

I felt a tickle on my wrist and looked down through the dim light. A wood spider as big as a jar top was settling on the back of my hand. I almost swooned, but Laura was still grasping on to my other arm. I lightly shook my hand to dislodge the spider, but it was bent on relaxing there. Its legs lightly scratched on my skin as if it were petting me.

I grabbed hold of my tenuous sanity and made one violent flick of my wrist. The spider shot from behind the plywood and into the room where the skinheads and tour participants were having their standoff. The poor spider bolted toward the group.

"Jeezus Christ!" one of the skinheads bellowed. Members of the tour group started shrieking. The huge spider had disrupted everything. It sounded like everyone was scrambling to escape the spider, but we could only see the rotten plywood and floor from our vantage point.

One of the skinheads shouted, "Let's go, Barrie. They must've gone this way. I want out of this freak show."

"Calm down, everyone. It was just a spider. Calm down," the guide was bawling to his patrons.

Laura leaned into me and whispered, "I think we should just stay here for a while."

Reliving the crawling spider on my hand, I said, "Easy for you to say." But I didn't move.

We waited until the tour group beat it out of the chamber. I peeked around the board into the gloom of the underground room. "I think everyone's gone for now. Any suggestions about what we should do?"

Laura looked out her side of the plywood and confirmed for herself that we were alone for the time being. "I think we should stay here, just not behind that board, until we can be sure we aren't being hunted. We'll probably have to duck behind that plywood a few more times because there's bound to be another tour or two passing this way. It's only midafternoon." Overhead, the boom of a large truck hitting a pothole disturbed the grave silence. We paced around the room for fifteen minutes before we had to hide again.

"Be careful, folks, and follow me." Another tour guide was bringing her group into the Underground. Without speaking, we squeezed behind the plywood again. I carefully took Laura's casted hand and we waited in the clammy space behind the plywood. I silently willed all spiders away from our little hidey place.

The tour guide spewed most of the same information the previous guide had so wittily delivered. However, this one put a more intellectual spin on the Underground history. I supposed her listeners felt more culturally satisfied than the previous group. When her lecture about the sofa was over and the group had stared gape-jawed at the dirt and cobwebs, they shuffled dutifully to the next stop on their tour without asking a single question.

Two more tours passed through, each one forcing us to scurry back to our shadowy hideout. I was beginning to feel like that traumatized spider I'd encountered earlier, trying to hide every time the humans passed through. When it was late in the afternoon, the tours stopped coming. There was no light coming through the glass sidewalk that made up sections of the ceiling. Evening had fallen upon Seattle. Laura and I huddled together on the dusty red sofa. We decided to wait a few hours longer in the Underground darkness, hoping that Dwight's men would give up the downtown search.

"Plus, we're probably locked in here. I really need to pee, Dev. What should I do? I can't see that well." Just then the security lights clicked on, such as they were. They were dim green lights lining the wall near the board walkway. At least we could see each other.

"Go pee behind the plywood. I'm never going to hide behind that thing again." I was starting to get itchy. "There's probably enough mold in here to crash my entire immune system. And I don't even want to think of the rats." I regretted saying the R-word the minute it came out of my mouth.

"Rats! That's right. Oh, yuck. I hate rats, Dev. How can I go pee now?" She huddled close to me on the couch, as if I could protect her from underground vermin.

"C'mon, we'll walk down the boardwalk a little ways, and you can pee off the edge. I'll even join you." We shuffled about a hundred feet down the walkway, pulled our pants down, and relieved ourselves. It was a refreshing moment.

Just as we'd returned to the red couch, music started playing. Both of us jumped and ran toward Laura's bag where the music came from.

"Your phone's on! Damn it, Dev. You left your phone on. They could track us." Laura had a hand on her hip and was berating me like an ornery schoolteacher.

"Hey, it's in your bag. You're the one who lifted it from my bedroom."

We stared down at the bag that sat innocently on the red sofa playing "Toxic" by Britney Spears. Laura looked at me in bewilderment. "'Toxic'?"

I shrugged. "You expected klezmer music?"

The phone stopped playing "Toxic" before I could answer it. Laura and I looked at each other in silent question about whether I should return the call.

"I'll just check and see if there's a message," I said. There was. Fitch.

"Who knew it snows in Colorado in October? My flight was postponed several times today, but I'm finally taking off in an hour. I'm turning this phone off now. Sorry about the delay. I won't get home till late, late, late. Where are you, anyway? Call me. We got a busy day tomorrow, Devy." I flinched at the "Devy" and closed my phone.

"That was Fitch. My researcher, the one who verified the bombing of the clinic in Colorado."

"Can she come get us? I really don't want to spend the night down here, Dev. Not with the natural inhabitants of this ecosystem and not with the ghosts probably lurking in corners." Laura cast an edgy look around.

"I'm not sure we have any choice. Fitch is stuck in Denver, at least for a little while, and I'm not sure who we can trust at this point. The wormy fingers of a U.S. senator can reach into places unavailable to us mere civilians." I turned my phone off, probably too late to avoid getting traced.

"Should we just go back to the entrance and try to break out? Maybe someone will hear us and let us out."

"The street's probably not safe. I think we should sit here for a few hours and wait. Just before morning, we'll either bust down the locked Underground Tour entrance or punt and call the police."

"You know the Stratton crowd has already weaseled its way into the Seattle Police Department. They are not a safe bet." Laura sat next to me and cradled her wrist. I wrapped my arm around her and pulled her close. She felt like the only stable and certain thing in the world.

She cuddled closer. "Will I ever be warm again?"

We leaned back into the sofa. "I'm getting a small hint of what it was like for my relatives as they hid in basements and crawlspaces, worried the Gestapo would find them. And my chances are better than theirs were." Hopelessness started to crowd my enjoyment of Laura's body next to mine.

"Hey, you're right. Our chances are far better, sweetheart. Stratton's party hasn't the power of the Gestapo, even though it wishes it had. We'll get out of this, and we'll tell the world what we know. I have the proof of her abortion. Maybe there will be no direct connection between her and the clinic bombing, but with the other deaths, there is a compelling case for her and Greenfield's culpability in this...this madness." Laura started to gently cry.

"Honey, what's wrong? Hey, you're my rock. Don't get all crumbly on me now." I took her shoulders and looked into her eyes.

Laura wiped her tears. "Maybe Elizabeth and I happened a decade ago, but I did love her. And even though the relationship is long over, some of that love is still there. It exists within me. Once I love someone, I always love that person. I'm not ashamed of that. It's how my heart works." She looked to me as if she needed understanding. "I don't want to hurt Elizabeth, but I have to remind myself that she's different now. And... my heart...it's looking in a different direction." Laura and her capacity for love, she was marvelous.

"Laura, maybe on some level, your love for Elizabeth will be what saves her. I truly believe she does not want to be the monster she's become. She was programmed early on for power, but her emotions have sometimes thwarted her programming. Witness her unplanned relationship with you. She may not know it consciously, but she wants to be stopped. I felt her ambivalence the night I did that reading for her. The night I first saw you." I pulled Laura into me, feeling the preciousness and mystery of our connection.

We lay quietly for a while.

Then Laura sat up and straddled my lap. "My wrist hurts and I'm trapped with thousands of rats," she said, "but I can only think of one thing to do to pass the time." She leaned in and kissed me, her mouth open and searching. No buildup or fumbling around, only a furnace of raw desire. I was surprised, but I wasn't going to fight her off.

Like when we made love at Tranquility, she worked the band out of my hair as if threading her hand through my locks was a crucial pleasure ingredient. She moaned into my mouth, making my belly grip and quiver. My center began throbbing, insistent in its craze to make me wet and ready for her.

"How do you do this to me?" I was gasping, mindless of our appalling surroundings.

"I should ask you the same question." Her voice caught as small tremors began shuddering through her. She took nips and sucks beneath my ear and moved down my neck to my shoulders. Then she licked her way back up to my ear where her lips made me lose all control when she whispered, "I want it. I want you. Now, Dev."

If I ever had any illusion that attorneys were tight and staid, it disappeared when Laura pushed me onto my back on that dusty sofa and ordered, "Pants down."

I kicked off my shoes, pledging to myself that my feet would not touch that gritty floor. Then I worked off my yoga pants and settled back, waiting for her direction. Laura, on her knees and straddling my legs, gazed at my panties for a long moment.

"I have a secret," she said. Her voice was husky. "I fantasize about sex in strange places."

"Let's make it more than a fantasy." I fought to catch my breath. I was in flagrant need of her. "Do what you want to me."

She hooked her finger into the waistband of my panties and

took her time pulling them down. She studied me and ran her hand along my belly. "Touch yourself. The way you like it."

Touching myself is something I happen to be pretty good at. I obliged her. As she watched my gradual loss of control, her breathing became ragged. Her hand dipped under her own waistband, and her rhythm matched mine.

I managed to demand, "Show me."

She removed her hand and pushed her sweats down so the string top pushed against my legs. She wore light coral bikinis with a narrow edge of lace. She fingered the band for a few moments and watched me crave to see more. She pulled the panties low enough so I could see her fingers enter her. That sight was so sexy, I came in gripping fury. My head and ears pounded with the rhythmic rush kneading my body. When the waves of passion subsided, I turned my attention to Laura.

"Take those off and come here." I have no idea how she removed her pants so quickly. It seemed only a few seconds before her wet center hovered over my face and then lowered to my mouth. It was the sweetest drink I ever had. And it took only a few strokes of my tongue before she came in my mouth, full and hard. Her nectar trickled from my lips.

The aroma of Laura's climax didn't sate me. I needed more. So I held her in place and tasted her until she came again. This time her legs quivered so violently that I allowed her to ease herself down and lie atop me. I wrapped my legs around her to keep her warm. We dozed, gorged and spent.

Later, we awoke and made love another tender time. Then we clothed ourselves to ward off the cool damp of the Underground.

"Laura, you know I don't want to leave you after this is all over, don't you?" I said, hoping she wouldn't be frightened by my second, albeit indirect, declaration of love.

"It's like you said, Dev. We are *bashert*." She nuzzled her head on my shoulder and settled onto my frame to make herself as comfortable as possible. "Now, love, I need to drift away for a while."

"Be my guest, Laura." Her breathing deepened. She twitched a few times, then fell into sound sleep.

❖

"Damsel, you have had coitus?" Pento was gazing down at me while I lay on the beach in the squeaky sand.

"Do I ever get to enter this place on my feet?" I struggled to standing. "And what makes you think I've had coitus, uh, sex?"

"I can feel your satisfaction, but you have an empty stomach. It growls." He was right about that. I hadn't eaten since the flank steak, whenever that was. Days? Hours? I was losing track of time.

"Tell me about Laura, Pento."

"She is an innocent." He cocked his helmeted head to the side as if I should know what he was talking about.

"I'm not sure what you mean." If he knew about the past hour I'd spent with Laura, I wondered if he would still call her "innocent."

"Her line carries the love that the Lady wishes to bestow on the world. Her line does not deal in power, subterfuge, or politics. The line of innocents is charged with compassion. It is an unfortunate line." He looked so sad.

"Wait, you lost me there. You just said they carry compassion and love. What could be so unfortunate about that?"

"Oh, the innocents are mostly misunderstood. Some are

blamed for others' mistakes. I think your word is scapegoated. Some are great teachers, but their teachings eventually become distorted by their students. Innocents are philanthropists who become reviled by the very people they help. Innocents like your Laura work for justice and often see their efforts sour with the human desire for retribution.

"However, damsel, innocents make the small changes, the changes that make the biggest difference. A single act of love has far-ranging effects that we cannot predict."

"What about an act of violence or cruelty? Don't those have far-ranging effects too?" Pento was making sense to me for once.

"Yes, if they are not responded to by an act of love. An act of cruelty must have a loving response or the act will have a life of its own. The kinds of loving responses that neutralize cruelty most humans are capable of choosing, but the innocent cannot choose. The innocent has only one response, determined love."

"Does Laura know about this? Has she been groomed too?"

"She is called innocent for a good reason. She only knows that she loves inordinately. It frightens her sometimes, her enormous capacity for compassion. And other humans assume it is a weakness, a failing of character. But there is one thing that should not be forgotten about the innocents: their love makes them ferocious. It is the paradox of the innocent. They can fight cruelty with a ferocity that can frighten even the strongest opponent."

"What is my role in all this, Pento?"

"To remain true to what you know and your purpose. And to assist Laura, the innocent. Your skills will complement her, making your union a powerful antidote to the Malignity.

Together, you have already restored some balance to the world. Your current task is nearly complete. Look around." He swept his hand, directing my attention to the Theater.

At first, everything had its usual facsimile characteristic. But as I watched, the sand dunes started to wither, almost curl into themselves. The sea stopped abruptly its wave action and crackled as it too withered. Sea birds folded like paper and drifted into the diminishing water.

"So I'll not see the Theater anymore, or you, Pento?" Something in me was cracking too, but it felt like grief.

"Damsel, I never leave you. Why do you think you are so good at meddling? Will we meet like this again, in the Theater? I cannot say. The Lady may need to deter the Malignity again in your lifetime." He paused and smiled his false teeth smile. "Have you noticed? The Priestess has stopped calling you. You are her champion, but she can never show gratitude. It does not exist within her. She is a mystery. In the meantime, the Malignity will continue to exert its will wherever humans choose to delude themselves."

"Wait, they help the Malignity with their delusions? Why must they continue? Can't they be stopped permanently?" Every time I thought I understood Pento, he would say something to refute that impression.

"It is as I said before. The Malignity is necessary, but it also needs balance. Humans make choices. Embracing compassion is a choice, but so is embracing delusion in all its manifestations. The very nature of human experience is choice. But you need to have the variety of choices apparent to you. When the Malignity gets too powerful, humans lose choices, compassionate choices among others. That cannot be allowed.

"I and the others like me are tasked with keeping choice

balanced for humans, but sometimes we fight amongst ourselves. We do not always agree on how much is too much. Do you see, damsel?"

"As above, so below?" I would ponder this conversation for a long time.

"That is correct. You finally understand. You are an able pupil." He did look proud of me, even if I was still baffled by much of his explanation. I had one more question before he completely dismantled the Theater.

"Pento, the key, what is the key to the Theater?"

"The 'key,' damsel?"

"Yeah, to this place. To the Theater. To you. What made me cross over?"

"That is easy. When it is necessary, members of the bloodlines can enter this realm only when they feel an emotion that is new to them. In your case, the emotional portal was outrage for another person's suffering. It was a feeling unknown to you at any depth. Often, people from the meddler line are disconnected from that particular emotion. The Lady helped instill that into you at the right times. To feel a new emotion opens doors. But that is a lengthy explanation, I fear." He cocked his head like a bird, as if listening.

"Damsel, we are running out of time in your realm. You must return to your Laura. This present task is almost complete. However, I must show you one more thing. Behold." He pointed behind me.

I turned just in time to duck. The cold-eyed Knight of Swords whipped a thick, gnarled staff at me. He took another swipe, making a scratching noise as it displaced the phony air. I jumped back. He missed me again, barely.

I backed away from his maniacal swings, the staff getting closer each time it passed my face. A rock in the process of dissolving tripped me onto my back. The knight became triumphant. He had me. His helmet morphed into Tom Dwight's bald head. With a raving growl, he brought the staff over his head and swung it toward my face.

Crack. It hit the ground next to my head. Something made him miss. He toppled sideways. I looked around for a weapon and saw I was back in Underground Seattle. Dwight had a dented two-by-four wrapped in his behemoth hand. He grabbed my leg and pulled me across the floor toward him. His mouth was frothing in rage. He aimed to smash me with the board.

Laura's leg stepped into my view of Dwight's berserk face. I heard him howl and his legs kicked in rabid lunacy. Laura moved away to reveal Dwight's gored face. The three wicked fingers of my garden tool were deeply embedded in his cheek and eye socket. Laura had knocked Dwight down and impaled him with my new Japanese cuttlefish hoe.

Dwight was twitching and not getting up. The finger of the tool that pierced his eye must have penetrated to the brain.

I crawled to Laura, whose eyes had the glare of a mother tiger protecting her young. Ferocious was the only word to describe her.

"C'mon, baby, we're getting out of here," she said. She snatched the board out of Dwight's quivering hand, grabbed her bag, and started toward the entrance of the Underground Tour. She walked like a warrior, swinging that board next to her leg. The stylish but run-down bag hanging off her casted wrist struck me as funny. I didn't care. She was my hero, and I would follow her anywhere.

The security lighting led us back along the plank walkway to the dented, paint-chipped door that would take us into the putrid alley and downtown Seattle. Laura stopped in front of the door, then handed me the hefty board.

"I can't do this one, Dev. Not one-handed like…like I did him back there." Tears welled in her now-remorseful eyes.

"Don't, Laura. Don't do that to yourself. He was worse than an animal. Think how many lives you saved by ridding the world of him. Mine, for one."

"It'll still take years of therapy to get over it." She nodded toward the door. "Go for it, sweetheart, and get me out of here." Then she sat on the edge of the walkway and buried her face in her hand.

I studied the door before battering it several times with the board. It was solid, probably metal cored, with an impenetrable lock outside. Its ramshackle appearance was a ruse to make tourgoers believe they were entering an authentically decrepit adventure. The lock was probably designed to keep the street riffraff from using the tour sights as a flophouse and urinal.

"Hand me my cell phone, honey. It's time we broke cover." I turned on the phone and dialed Fitch.

"Finally, Devy. I've been waiting all night, and my back's killing me." I could tell Fitch was happier to hear from me than she was cranky.

"We need a pickup. The Underground Tour entrance near First and Occidental. Know it?"

"Know it? I'm three minutes away."

"How?" Here came another Fitch-as-genius story.

"Deduction. You weren't at Tranquility. I hacked the phones at your security company. Those boys were freakin' out. They thought you'd been burglarized, maybe kidnapped, and they'd be liable. All your doors were unlocked, lights on, and your car was vandalized. Like mine."

Tom Dwight probably did that when he couldn't hit us with bullets, I thought. Malicious bastard.

"So they eventually tracked you to some pilot named

Haney. For a security company, they sure have woefully unsecure cell phones."

"I'll be sure to put that in their annual customer satisfaction survey."

"Right. Anyhow, old Haney said he dropped you two off at south Lake Union. Brilliant call hiring a pilot, by the way. Old Haney said you girls were talking about getting to a bank. That's when I had to get in my car."

"Why is that?"

"You weren't at your condo, and I was sure Laura's place wasn't safe. So you had to be roaming around downtown somewhere. The clubs were closing by the time I got there. First thing I saw scouting Pioneer Square were the two fuckhead Nazis I ran into out on Lopez. The ones who harassed me and axed my Jag's passenger seat. Um, I think your car got the same treatment. Sorry."

"Doesn't matter. So where are you now?"

A screaming metallic crash shook the door. I dropped the phone. I hurled myself against the wall and got ready to plant that board right into the face of a skinhead. Ripping metal screeched outside the door. It flew open. The black silhouette was holding a huge double-bladed axe. I swung the board with every ounce of my strength, but he jerked his head back. A complete miss.

"Jeezus H. Kee-riste, Rosten, it's me. Told ya I was good with an axe." Fitch stepped into the murky security light and held up the axe. "I hacked those locks clean off the door."

"Goddamn, you have no idea how close you came to losing your brains. You should have identified yourself." My chest was heaving from the adrenaline and the effort of swinging the board. Laura sat there with her mouth half-open, glancing between the two of us.

"Laura, honey, meet Fitch. Fitch, this is Laura Bishop." I sounded more grudging than I should have. But Fitch had scared me. She probably got a thrill out of it too. Sadists are difficult friends sometimes.

Laura and Fitch shook hands like they were at a networking meet and greet, then they took measure of each other. Both of them nodded at the same time, and I knew a fresh alliance was born.

"Okay, ladies, my newly repaired car is outside for your rescue convenience. Let's go before the camo-boys come after us." Fitch turned and swaggered out the door but stopped a few feet out. She turned to us, her eyes hard, and put her index finger to her lips. Then she motioned for us to follow her. I peeked out the door and saw the two goons standing at the far end of the alley, trying to figure out who we were.

Fitch made hurry-up motions, so I pulled Laura into the alley with me. The car was idling about twenty feet away. We made a desperate dash and hauled ourselves in. Fitch was in the driver's seat while Laura and I sprawled in the plush backseat.

The skinheads were running into the headlight beams. I don't think the boys were very bright. They showed no caution. Fitch hammered her accelerator and plowed into them. Their bodies thunked onto the hood and one rolled over the roof. I looked back to see both men writhing around in the oily muck that covered the pavement.

Fitch drove to the end of the alley and into the empty street, where she turned her Jaguar around and reentered the alley. Both men were lying together on the left side, their legs protruding into the center. It was the easiest thing. Fitch calmly drove over all four legs and smirked as the skinheads screamed.

"Dev, I think you should call the police on our two boys

back there. Too bad we don't know where Dwight is," Fitch said.

"We know where he is. The police are going to get their murderers in a one-stop shop today. Such a bargain." I felt Laura tremble next to me. I held and soothed her while she soaked my shirt with her tears. I knew it would be a long time before Laura wouldn't cry every time she remembered this one insane week.

My beautiful Laura and her beautiful heart.

CHAPTER FIFTEEN

The Talmud reminds us that if we save one person, it's as if we have saved the world.

My Laura saved the world several times that day in October. More innocent people would have died, many more.

Later that morning, Laura appeared in front of the press. The conference was held in the boardroom of my bank. Laura's attorney stood nearby, as did several security guards who worked for the bank.

Fitch had fashioned a slide show with the photos I'd taken of Laura's scrapbook. With each slide, Laura related her history with Elizabeth Stratton. When she revealed that she and Elizabeth had been lovers, the press murmured. But when she exposed that Stratton had had an abortion at a clinic that was now destroyed, the room exploded. In those few minutes, the Malignity was stalled in its plans for Stratton and Greenfield.

The power structure behind Elizabeth Stratton was cruel and ruthless. There was nothing religious about Elizabeth Stratton and Jerry Greenfield. They were tools of the Malignity. A bloodline bred for despotic power.

But as any parent can attest, children don't become the

people parents plan them to be. Stratton's ability to feel love was not in the Malignity's plans for her. Her love for Laura was her weakness in the eyes of the Malignity and all its henchmen.

After authorities verified the bombers of the abortion clinic were attached to the Stratton campaign, they redirected their investigation into the murders at Smith Tower. They were not able to make a strong enough connection between the two events, but enough circumstantial evidence gave the starry-eyed Stratton minions pause. Most Strattonites dropped their support for Senator Stratton, waking up as if they had been in an extended opium dream.

Elizabeth Stratton retired from the public eye. She cited the desire to spend time praying and meditating. Oy.

Elizabeth's husband, Jerry Greenfield, was charged with all kinds of conspiracies and began mounting endless legal resistance to the inevitable, but he continued to preach to a greatly diminished but still wild-eyed flock.

Tom Dwight didn't die. He was sent to a maximum-security federal penitentiary for the criminally insane where he sits all day drooling. His two buddies hobble their way to their prison showers and look over their shoulders.

Laura is healing. Her law practice thrives, but she takes only cases that can help the vulnerable. She is a hero to most people, but she still gets death threats from disappointed Strattonites. She will need a bodyguard indefinitely.

I get to cook for her every evening. When she comes home after work, the peace and comfort we feel together is a balm to both of us. My immune system has never been stronger.

And the Malignity? It's still around. We all grapple with it every day to keep it from overwhelming us. We see it when people spit hate at others for being different. We see it in grim countries that torture their women and children. We see it in the raving killer who guns down innocent people going about their business. It's the eternal human struggle. My work as a meddler isn't over. I expect to hear from Pento any time now.

About the Author

Kristin Marra spent the first thirty-five years of her life in Montana, where she never learned to love snow. Conceding defeat, she moved to Seattle and freely admits she adores the clouds and gloom. As far as Kristin is concerned, overcast days encourage delightfully obscene hours of reading and more hours for writing. Besides books, cooking, and movies, Kristin enjoys sharing adventures with her beloved partner Judith, world-class daughter Rachel, and loyal dog Spud. Kristin is currently working on the sequel to her first novel, *Wind and Bones*. She is happily employed in the education field.

Books Available From Bold Strokes Books

Darkness Embraced by Winter Pennington. Surrounded by harsh vampire politics and secret ambitions, Epiphany learns that an old enemy is plotting treason against the woman she once loved, and to save all she holds dear, she must embrace and form an alliance with the dark. (978-1-60282-221-4)

78 Keys by Kristin Marra. When the cosmic powers choose Devorah Rosten to be their next gladiator, she must use her unique skills to try to save her lover, herself, and even humankind. (978-1-60282-222-1)

Playing Passion's Game by Lesley Davis. Trent Williams's only passion in life is gaming—until Juliet Sullivan makes her realize that love can be a whole different game to play. (978-1-60282-223-8)

Retirement Plan by Martha Miller. A modern morality tale of justice, retribution, and women who refuse to be politely invisible. (978-1-60282-224-5)

Who Dat Whodunnit by Greg Herren. Popular New Orleans detective Scotty Bradley investigates the murder of a dethroned beauty queen to clear the name of his pro football–playing cousin. (978-1-60282-225-2)

The Company He Keeps by Dale Chase. A riotously erotic collection of stories set in the sexually repressed and therefore sexually rampant Victorian era. (978-1-60282-226-9)

Cursebusters! by Julie Smith. Budding-psychic Reeno is the most accomplished teenage burglar in California, but one tiny screw-up and poof!—she's sentenced to Bad Girl School. And that isn't even her worst problem. Her sister Haley's dying of an illness no one can diagnose, and now she can't even help. (978-1-60282-559-8)

True Confessions by PJ Trebelhorn. Lynn Patrick finally has a chance with the only woman she's ever loved, her lifelong friend Jessica Greenfield, but Jessie is still tormented by an abusive past. (978-1-60282-216-0)

Jane Doe by Lisa Girolami. On a getaway trip to Las Vegas, Emily Carver gambles on a chance for true love and discovers that sometimes in order to find yourself, you have to start from scratch. (978-1-60282-217-7)

Ghosts of Winter by Rebecca S. Buck. Can Ros Wynne, who has lost everything she thought defined her, find her true life—and her true love—surrounded by the lingering history of the once-grand Winter Manor? (978-1-60282-219-1)

Who I Am by M.L. Rice. Devin Kelly's senior year is a disaster. She's in a new school in a new town, and the school bully is making her life miserable—but then she meets his sister Melanie and realizes her feelings for her are more than platonic. (978-1-60282-231-3)

Call Me Softly by D. Jackson Leigh. Polo pony trainer Swain Butler finds that neither her heart nor her secret are safe when beautiful British heiress Lillie Wetherington arrives to bury her grandmother, Swain's employer. (978-1-60282-215-3)

Split by Mel Bossa. Weeks before Derek O'Reilly's engagement party, a chance meeting with Nick Lund, his teenage first love, catapults him into the past, where he relives that powerful relationship revealing what he and Nick were, still are, and might yet be to each other. (978-1-60282-220-7)

Blood Hunt by L.L. Raand. In the second Midnight Hunters Novel, Detective Jody Gates, heir to a powerful Vampire clan, forges an uneasy alliance with Sylvan, the Wolf Were Alpha, to battle a shadow army of humans and rogue Weres, while fighting her growing hunger for human reporter Becca Land. (978-1-60282-209-2)

Loving Liz by Bobbi Marolt. When theater actor Marty Jamison turns diva and Liz Chandler walks out on her, Marty must confront a cheating lover from the past to understand why life is crumbling around her. (978-1-60282-210-8)

Kiss the Rain by Larkin Rose. How will successful fashion designer Eve Harris react when she discovers the new woman in her life, Jodi, and her secret fantasy phone date, Lexi, are one and the same? (978-1-60282-211-5)

Sarah, Son of God by Justine Saracen. In a story within a story within a story, a transgendered beauty takes us through Stonewall-rioting New York, Venice under the Inquisition, and Nero's Rome. (978-1-60282-212-2)

Sleeping Angel by Greg Herren. Eric Matthews survives a terrible car accident only to find out everyone in town thinks he's a murderer—and he has to clear his name even though he has no memories of what happened. (978-1-60282-214-6)

Dying to Live by Kim Baldwin & Xenia Alexiou. British socialite Zoe Anderson-Howe's pampered life is abruptly shattered when she's taken hostage by FARC guerrillas while on a business trip to Bogota, and Elite Operative Fetch must rescue her to complete her own harrowing mission. (978-1-60282-200-9)

Indigo Moon by Gill McKnight. Hope Glassy and Godfrey Meyers are on a mercy mission to save their friend Isabelle after she is attacked by a rogue werewolf—but does Isabelle want to be saved from the sexy wolf who claimed her as a mate? (978-1-60282-201-6)

Parties in Congress by Colette Moody. Bijal Rao, Indian-American moderate Independent, gets the break of her career when she's hired to work on the congressional campaign of Janet Denton—until she meets her remarkably attractive and charismatic opponent, Colleen O'Bannon. (978-1-60282-202-3)

The Collectors by Leslie Gowan. Laura owns what might be the world's most extensive collection of BDSM lesbian erotica, but that's as close as she's gotten to the world of her fantasies. Until, that is, her friend Adele introduces her to Adele's mistress Jeanne—art collector, heiress, and experienced dominant. With Jeanne's first command, Laura's life changes forever. (978-1-60282-208-5)

Breathless, edited by Radclyffe and Stacia Seaman. Bold Strokes Books romance authors give readers a glimpse into the lives of favorite couples celebrating special moments "after the honeymoon ends." Enjoy a new look at lesbians in love or revisit favorite characters from some of BSB's best-selling romances. (978-1-60282-207-8)